# JEMIMA'S NOBLEMAN

1816: When her father's famous fan shop in the Strand is reduced to ashes, Jemima dons the clothing of a maid and moves with him to the docklands of London — and is present at an accident where William, Earl of Swanington, almost literally falls into her lap! But William is fleeing from accusations that he's murdered a servant — and when he sees the beautiful Jemima at a Society ball, he wonders if she's the one who robbed him after his accident! Can true love blossom in such circumstances?

*Books by Anne Holman*
*in the Linford Romance Library:*

SAIL AWAY TO LOVE
HER HEART'S DESIRE
FLYING TO HEAVEN
FINDING LOVE
HIDDEN LOVE
SECRET LOVE
CAPTURED LOVE
THE LONGMAN GIRL
THE OWNER OF THORPE HALL
THE CAPTAIN'S MESSENGER
BELLE OF THE BALL
CASSIE'S FAVOUR
THE GOLDEN DOLLY
A NEW LIFE FOR ROSEMARY
VERA'S VICTORY
FOLLIES HOTEL
VERA'S VALOUR
THE TREASURE SEEKERS
IN HER SHOES
VERA'S VENTURE
THE ART OF LOVE
THE SIGNET RING

ANNE HOLMAN

# JEMIMA'S NOBLEMAN

*Complete and Unabridged*

## LINFORD
*Leicester*

First published in Great Britain in 2018

First Linford Edition
published 2019

A catalogue record for this book is available
from the British Library.

ISBN 978–1–4448–4290–6

Published by
F. A. Thorpe (Publishing)
Anstey, Leicestershire

Set by Words & Graphics Ltd.
Anstey, Leicestershire
Printed and bound in Great Britain by
T. J. International Ltd., Padstow, Cornwall

This book is printed on acid-free paper

# 1

*London 1816*

'We're done for, daughter! We have lost everything!'

On hearing this anguished cry from her father and seeing his stricken expression through the billowing smoke, Miss Jemima Perrot screamed!

Backing away from the intense heat and roaring flames of the fire with the raucous crowd who'd come to view the spectacle, Jemima felt helpless to do anything to prevent her father's famous fan shop in the Strand from being reduced to ashes.

Even the London Fire Brigade, with its loud clanging bell, came too late to save any of the valuable Chinese merchandise, as the crackling fire roared skywards.

However, she'd no time to stand and stare at her home being burned — she had to find her poor father . . . Ah, there he was, looking devasted. Despite her anguish, Jemima must make an effort to help him with his overwhelming loss.

'Papa,' she said, as she put an arm around his drooping shoulders. 'At least we've not been burned — and some of your staff may have been injured but no one has been killed or badly hurt.'

Seeing him look up bleakly as he wiped away dirt and sweat from his scorched face with his handkerchief, she feared her words were inadequate to comfort him.

Jemima realised that her father suddenly saw himself as a ruined man. From being a proud businessman, well-respected and wealthy, owning a classical styled property, he'd become one the many poor people in the great city of London.

His shop had been the haunt of fashionable ladies wanting fine, decorative accessories. Ladies liked to come and peer through the sash windows, excited to see the intricately carved ivory fans, decorated by the finest fan painters in China — but now his exquisite collection had gone for ever, up in smoke!

Jemima trembled, hardly believing the disaster could have happened so fast.

Earlier that afternoon she had been in their house, upstairs over the shop, when the alarm was raised. Below, the kitchen fire had suddenly become out of control. Giant flames licking around the roast on the spit had caught an oven cloth alight, and soon the kitchen was ablaze.

The screaming maids had fled as the fire quickly travelled from the kitchen into the shop and no one could stop it.

Jemima had flown downstairs into the shop where her father was trying to extinguish the flames from his valuable property. Over the sound of splitting timbers and crashing beams, together with the screams of his servants and shop assistants, she begged him to leave the premises immediately.

Jemima and her father stood together

outside the burning embers of the building on the pavement with the gathering crowd, coughing and blinking sore eyes as they were enveloped with grey smoke that billowed around, watching their home and livelihood become a furnace.

'Alas, we are now little more than beggars!' moaned Mr Perrot, covering his face with his soot-smeared hands.

'Not entirely, Papa!' Jemima contradicted, knowing she had now, at the age of twenty-five, to take care of her distraught parent, who was rocking, shaking his head and wringing his hands in a helpless fashion. She must overcome her shock and appear calm, and yet inside, Jemima felt a void of despair. All her worldly goods had been destroyed because she'd had no time to save anything. Her beautiful clothes and furniture, her precious collection of jewellery that had belonged to her late Mama had all gone. Tears she couldn't control trickled down her cheeks.

'What are we going to do?'

Her father's question made Jemima

start. With a gulp, she cast aside her feelings of hopelessness. She had to think immediately of a way for them to survive — other than to beg in the streets. She said the first thing that came into her head. 'We'll go to my old school friend, Sylvia Smithson, and ask her parents for assistance. They live not far away. We can walk there.'

Jemima took her father's arm and pulled him away from the piles of dying embers that had been his home and famous shop, saying, 'Sylvia's father is a rich alderman and has room for guests in his house, and her mother is a charming lady.'

Mr Perrot had friends too, merchants and business acquaintances nearby, but they were too grand, and he was too devastated, to go knocking on their doors asking for help.

Turning away from their destroyed home, Jemma went over their situation in her mind.

Mr Perrot's wife, Jemima's mama, had died several years ago, and although they had one son, he was far away buying new fan merchandise in China and was not due back for some time.

'If only your brother, Charles, was here!' Mr Perrot kept repeating fretfully as he plodded along the street with downcast head.

Jemima wished it too. In a nightmare of grief, and feeling as shaky as her father, she was doing her best not to break down as they continued walking with heavy hearts through the streets towards the Smithson's house.

They now had nothing left from the comfortable life she had enjoyed and her father had worked so hard to achieve. A few savings in the bank and the clothes they wore — that was all.

\* \* \*

Miss Sylvia Smithson, Jemma thought, had better looks than sense. Her life, in some ways very like Jemima's had been, was as a rather spoilt only daughter.

Miss Smithson's only consideration was which of her pretty dresses to wear, dainties to eat, and admirers to flirt with when she went to balls. Nevertheless, Jemima liked Sylvia as she was a sweet-natured girl.

Sylvia and her parents were sympathetic seeing the distraught father and daughter who arrived that evening. Mr and Mrs Smithson willingly offered destitute Jemima and her papa their condolences and made them welcome.

★　★　★

The next morning the girls chatted while they were dressing in Sylvia's boudoir.

Jemima said, 'You and your parents have been so kind to us. Still, it's all very well you saying we can stay here but we can't. My Papa needs a home of his own. A business too.'

'I can't think why he can't just retire.'

'My father likes working. He's always been a shopkeeper and he'd be lost without a job.' How could Jemima explain what it was like to be suddenly without means? Seeing Sylvia's puzzled expression, Jemima added, 'Papa doesn't want to be beholden to anyone.'

Sylvia had little idea, being a wealthy young lady, what being destitute meant. As the young lady twirled in front of her standing mirror in one of her latest muslin day gowns, she said lightly, 'Well, you can stay here, Jemima — even if your father chooses to live in the poorhouse.'

Jemima blinked at her frivolous friend.

'Sylvia!' she gasped. 'I love my papa dearly. I could never abandon him!'

'I am sorry,' Sylvia said in a contrite voice. 'That was a callous thing for me to say. I love my parents and could not abandon them either.'

In silence the girls looked at each other. One was rich, and one was now poor, but they were still friends. Sylvia had generously given Jemima some of her clothes, and after all, Jemima told herself, she was only trying to comfort her.

Jemima frowned, saying, 'I've been thinking . . . '

Sylvia dabbed some expensive perfume on her wrists and neck. 'Would you like some?'

'Thank you,' Jemima replied as she dabbed a little on her wrists — but she was deeply worried. It was no use pretending she could continue to attire herself in ladies' gowns and smell like flowers when she now had to earn her living.

'I wonder,' she said slowly, 'if you could get me some maid's clothes?'

'Whatever for?' Sylvia's eyes sparkled. 'Is there a dressing up ball?'

Jemima smiled. 'No. I wish to disguise myself to be free to walk around London to look for an empty shop my father could use when my brother returns with more merchandise. Being dressed like a lady would not let me do so.'

Sylvia looked doubtful. 'Well, I dare say one of the maids could give you some of her cast-off things if I got her some new ones to replace them. But they would probably be very shabby and unpleasant to wear!'

'That would be ideal, as I wish to appear as if I am a poor working woman.'

Eyeing her friend, Sylvia conceded, 'I suppose if you cover yourself well — hide your lovely auburn hair — you could make yourself look like a maid.' Sylvia hasten to add, 'But it's risky. There are many rogues about in London.'

Jemima suspected Sylvia had no idea of the real dangers the cheaper side of London harboured. Although Jemima did not really know much about crime herself. At the age of twenty-five, she was not unaware of robbers, prostitutes and drunks, and she knew she couldn't expect to avoid seeing some of the poverty and evils that existed in London if she was to achieve her goal of finding an empty shop for her father.

'Mama would not like you walking the streets alone,' Sylvia continued, 'She always insists I'm accompanied by an older lady or a maid — even to visit the library not far from here.'

Jemima was unsurprised. If she were the mother of a very attractive but delightfully feather-brained daughter like Sylvia, she would be just as protective. But Jemima was made of sterner stuff. Having lost her own mama, she had fended for herself for years. She'd gone out alone shopping and managed the housekeeping efficiently too.

'Sylvia, I know my way around London better than you, and if I was dressed like a maid no one will turn to look at me. I shall be quite safe. I need to see if I can find a new business premises for Papa — however humble.'

'Well,' said Sylvia, who had finished her toilette and was ready to go downstairs for breakfast, 'rather you than me. I should not plan to do anything so adventurous. I simply hope a handsome rich man will ask me to marry him.'

'Yes indeed.' Jemima chuckled. 'Isn't that what all young ladies hope for?' Yet she was aware that a young woman in a

11

lowly position like herself might more likely be the victim of some London scoundrel than to find a rich husband. In truth, Jemima didn't feel nearly as confident as she pretended, but she felt she had to overcome her apprehension and face her new life of hardship boldly — hopefully it would only be temporary.

★   ★   ★

It happened by luck that Jemima heard about the pawn shop from a footman who happened to mention it in her hearing.

'I found this gold watch,' the footman was telling a colleague, 'and while I was looking for the owner . . . ' A likely story, thought Jemima, who knew finding meant keeping to the likes of him. 'I took it to a pawn shop in Gin Lane. Just in case I had to find it quickly, you understand.'

Jemima understood the footman could be hanged for having a superb gold watch that clearly didn't belong to him, but he would have some money in his pocket if he pawned it.

The other footman was impressed by the thieving footman's ingenuity.

'Anyhow, that pawn shop is for sale. Lock, stock and barrel for a few sovereigns — a good opportunity for someone wanting to make a living. But I ain't interested in dealing with people's old things. I've a good job here. A smart livery to wear, and a bed to sleep on and the cook gives us good meals,' explained the footman, then went on to chatter about other news.

Jemima, covered in a patched dress and drab cloak she'd borrowed from a maid, set off on the long walk down to the poorer area of London, by the docks, and inspected the pawn shop the men were talking about in Gin Lane.

* * *

'All England is abuzz with the news,' Alderman Smithson announced to his

13

wife and guests one evening putting down his newspaper.

It was after dinner as they sat drinking tea in his gracious drawing room.

'What is that?' asked Sylvia and her mother in unison, keen to hear the latest gossip.

Alderman Smithson pointed to the newspaper saying, 'The enormously rich young Earl of Swanington has been accused of killing one of his servants and is due to be hanged!'

A shocked silence fell, everyone wondering why a nobleman could have been so evil.

'When is the killer to die?' asked Sylvia, wide-eyed, as if relishing the story.

The Alderman replied, 'Why, when they catch him. He's on the run.'

Jemima couldn't help feeling sorry for the poor fugitive. No, she corrected herself. He was not poor, as she and her father were. He was probably able to hide himself with all the money at his disposal. He could easily pay for people to conceal him. Anyway, perhaps he had not committed murder — newspapers sometimes printed stories that were not always true to attract customers to buy them.

'Well, at least he is not bored!' said Mr Perrot with a loud sigh, which seemed a strange remark to everyone except Jemima. She understood her father's feeling of a big void in his life.

'Swanington . . . Swanington . . . let me think,' said Mrs Smithson. 'That is a vast estate in the West of England, I believe. There was some sort of a tragedy . . . Yes, I was told that the young man's parents were killed when he was a baby. William was brought up by his grandmother — a staunch lady, they say she is.'

'Staunch? That's a strange word to use, Mama,' cried Sylvia.

Indeed, it made Jemima raise her eyebrows.

Mrs Smithson took a sip of tea and replaced her cup and saucer on the small table by her chair. 'I heard,' she continued, 'that the Dowager Countess of Swanington — who rarely visits London these days — has been a good guardian, a real battler and — '

'Battler?' echoed Sylvia. 'Mama, that sounds an even worse description of the noble lady!'

'Well, the gossips say she is a proud lady and a good person but has some dreadful relatives. She has been protecting the boy from them.'

Alderman Smithson boomed, 'Made the lad into a namby-pamby, has she? Over-cosseted by his grandmother — allowed him to get into trouble. It certainly sounds as if he has — if he's killed a servant girl and hoofed it!'

Jemima felt compassionate for anyone who had suffered misfortune. She said what she thought aloud. 'The Earl must now be a grown man. And let us not forget, he has only been *accused* of murder — that is not the same as doing it!'

# 2

Jemima spoke to her father quietly when they were alone together. 'I do understand how hard it must be for you living here, accepting hospitality and feeling ashamed at having to be obliged to Sylvia's parents. And with too much time on your hands to think of the loss you have suffered, you feel utterly miserable.'

Mr Perrot nodded in agreement, so Jemima continued, 'So I have been thinking about how we should spend our time waiting for Charles to return. I've been out looking and I have found an empty shop premises for you.'

Her father's eyes flicked with interest, so Jemima went on, 'It's a pawn shop needing an owner. Although it's in the dockland and about as grimy as any shop you would find in London. However it has living space above the shop and we are used to that. I can clean it up. You can be behind a counter again, dealing with customers. And think of the service you'll be providing people who need ready cash.'

Mr Perrot smiled at the thought of being a shopkeeper again. He said, 'I have a little money in the bank, but I should give it to our kind hosts, not spend it on buying a shop.'

'You can send Mr and Mrs Smithson some money later when the shop is making a profit.'

'A pawn shop won't make much money, Jemima. We'll survive, but that's about all.'

'I know,' she pursed her lips, knowing their previous life of luxury was over, 'But it should tide us over until Charles comes home.'

'He may not.'

Jemima had to admit the possibility that her brother could marry and decide to stay in China.

'Don't think that, Papa! We may see Charles back any day. But in the meantime, some shop work will be of interest to you.'

Mr Perrot looked thoughtful, then nodded. 'Yes, I think you're right, m' dear. Now that I've got over my fall out of society, I feel ready to start a new business afresh, however lowly it is. But as you describe the shop it will not be suitable as your home, Jemima. I want you to stay here, living like a lady.'

'Papa, I won't leave you. I'm coming with you to look after you, cook your meals and do your washing like any working woman does.'

'But my child, you have no idea of the hard work these women are used to.'

'Fiddlesticks! I can learn.'

'There are dangers in poor neighbourhoods you know nothing of.'

Jemima accepted that was so but, determined to assist her father, she felt she was prepared to accept a life of poverty and possible danger, so she said, 'I would much rather work at looking after you than stay here as Sylvia's paid companion. She's kindness itself, but like you, I want to make my own life.'

Consequently, the next day, Mr Perrot went to Cheapside to visit the shop.

He inspected the pawned items and was fascinated to learn a new business.

Then he went to his bank and, withdrawing all the money he had, he bought the pawn shop.

He appeared satisfied, although he admitted to Jemima, 'The shop is in a rough district with all sorts of vagabonds around. We must take great care when we go out, especially you, young lady.'

Jemima gave her father a kiss, saying, 'I have already thought of that, Papa. I intend to dress like a maid.'

So, without saying anything about the poor state of the property to her kind host and hostess — or indeed to Sylvia — other than to say that she and her father had found somewhere to live, Mr Tom Perrot and Miss Jemima Perrot moved into Number Five, Gin Lane.

\* \* \*

The dockland people found it strange at first to find people of quality living among them, but they soon respected the Perrots because they were willing to help folk in desperate need.

The pawn shop thrived under Mr Perrot's experience of shop keeping — but his health did not. Living in a poor district, meeting some of the most unfortunate people anxious to pawn what they could for money to stay alive, the old gentleman caught a disease that made him ill and within a few months, it killed him.

Distraught, Jemima faced a dilemma.

Was she able to continue living in Gin Lane alone? The people she had grown to know round about in the deprived district were not unfriendly towards her as she put on no airs, and as she had been running the pawn shop since her father's illness she decided she may as well continue with it until her brother came home.

As her brother, Charles Perrot, had been addressing his correspondence to his father's old fan shop which had burned down, it never reached him. However, Jemima still lived in hope that one day he would come and rescue her, and she would be able to put the low life behind her and to return to the happy life of living like a lady.

Adjusted to her life of poverty, Jemima was not too unhappy. Reconciled to her father's death and knowing she had done what she could and having learned the pawnbroker's business with him, she was able to continue earning her living.

★   ★   ★

One Sunday, after visiting Sylvia, Jemima had a long way to walk back to her shop in Gin Lane. It was getting dark and there were no lamplights in the poorer districts — but fortunately moonlight.

A driver's horn blasted loud and clear in the evening air. Jemima gasped as she heard the loud clattering of horse's hooves behind her in the narrow road, and quickly stepped aside, sheltering in the safety of a doorway.

She knew respectable carriages didn't normally come along this narrow, dirty way — certainly not at speed in the wintertime gloom.

Suddenly, a large rat scurrying across the road made the carriage horses scream and rear. Startled, Jemima watched as the coach jolted violently, tipping a little before it lurched forward and was soon racing out of sight.

After the commotion was over, she noticed a passenger had fallen off the back of the carriage and was left behind lying on the ground.

However, she was not the only one who had seen the accident. Within minutes she lost sight of the prone body, because the local thieves and pickpockets surrounded it, like flies buzzing around a carcass. They made quick work of taking anything of value they could remove from the poor unconscious person!

Jemima could do nothing to prevent the victim from being robbed, because she was conscious of being alone, and although dressed like a maid, she didn't like being seen out when daylight faded into night time.

'Shoo! Be off with you!' Jemima rushed forward after the thieves had finished their evil work, driving off a few ragamuffin boys who'd crowded around like vultures to see if their elders had left any pickings for them to take from the hapless fellow.

Everyone vanished, leaving her alone with an injured man.

'I can't leave this poor fellow here!' she cried, admiring the man's youthful features and fashionably curled hair-style. Obviously, he was a gentleman as he was wearing quality clothes — what was left of them on him — and he'd probably had a great deal of money on him, all now gone. Even his boots and hat the thieves had stolen from the unfortunate victim!

Jemima had come closer bending

over the body and was relieved to see he was still breathing. 'Thank goodness!' she said.

*My, he's extremely good-looking!* Strangely, she thought she may have seen him before. Perhaps she'd met him as one of her brother's acquaintances years ago when she was able to live in the comfortable world of the middle class. Even with closed eyes and mud over his face there was something noble-looking about him.

She was not unaware of the man's physical shape either, in his state of semi-undress. And if she'd not been used to nursing her father before he died, a young lady like herself might have been embarrassed — but Jemima was not, and could only admire the well-formed male. She frowned, wondering what she could do to help him.

Jemima always liked to help anyone in distress if she could, but here was a heavy man lying in the middle of the highway — and another carriage could come bowling along at any minute. She hadn't the strength to drag him out of the way.

As she knelt by the victim she grimaced at the sight of blood oozing from a nasty gash on his head, trickling onto the filthy ground. She was horrified to think such a perfect specimen of manhood might bleed to death.

A low moan from him dispelled any fear that he was dying.

'Where am I? What am I doing here?'

His questions sounded sharp, as if he was giving orders, rather than requests for answers.

'I'll miss my ship. It sails with the tide at six.'

He tried to lift himself up but groaned as if in pain before he fell to the ground again and slipped back into unconsciousness.

Jemima used her handkerchief to blot the cut above his eye where the blood was running down his cheek. 'Quiet now,' she said as her hand stroked his face.

He opened his eyes as he raised his

head to look at her but soon fell back with another murmur of pain. Jemima's teeth clenched, wondering what she should do. He'd been stripped to his shift, and his battered body needed to be covered, but Jemima had barely enough to cover herself from the sharp wind that blew in from the sea on that November evening.

A bark made her look up and see a small dog trotting up, alternately barking and sniffing. Jemima smiled, giving the animal's furry head a stroke when he came close to her.

'Where's your master then, M'harty?'

'Right here, Jemima.'

Sure enough, the large blind man was lumbering along, tapping with his stick.

Jemima sighed with relief. Getting to her feet she called, 'Joe, I need your help to drag this injured man off the road.'

'I can't see no man,' Joe joked.

'If you keep walking you'll fall over him.'

'Hah! I've got him now.' Joe came up

and jabbed the body with his stick. 'Big un, ain't he?'

'Yes, indeed. He's a fair-sized man. That's why I can't move him.'

'How come he's lying here in the road?'

'I saw him fall off a coach racing to the docks.'

Joe prodded the prone figure with his cane again. 'Is he still alive?'

'Yes, Joe, he's alive, but he could be run over lying here. Or freeze to death on this cold night. We should put him somewhere safe, where he can recover.'

'And where in this vice-ridden neighbourhood do you think that might be, lass?'

Jemima frowned as she tried to think of somewhere.

'My pawn shop it will have to be,' she said decisively. 'It's not far from here and it's the only place I can think of. Quick now, let's move him before the body-snatchers get him on a slab for the physicians to carve him up!'

The fact that this stranger was too

fine a man to be sliced up by medical students was certainly one reason Jemima was determined to save him. But another was a more gut reaction — and a reaction she hardly dare acknowledge — that she saw him as a potential husband. Such thoughts from an unmarried young lady should be unthinkable, but she was now a woman with no reputation to worry about, having to survive by pawning goods in this disreputable neighbourhood. So she could indulge in her secret longing for a young man to love. And he definitely had the looks of the kind of man she fancied.

Fortunately, blind Joe was a tough ex-seaman and, once he had been given directions for moving the body, he had little difficulty hoisting the man over his shoulder and being guided by Jemima along to the dockside pawn shop where she lived.

Getting the blind man and his heavy load upstairs was more difficult, but with enough curses and yelps as Joe bumped himself, the unconscious man was laid on the bed in her late father's room.

'There now,' Joe panted with the exertion as he lay his burden down.

'I'll get water to sponge his face and hands.'

Occasionally, as Jemima washed him and covered his wounds with a healing balm, it seemed as if the injured stranger's eyes flickered open, before he closed them and appeared dead to the world again.

Having cleaned him and covered him with a blanket, they left him to sleep.

★ ★ ★

'That young man drank too much at the last post house most likely, and toppled off the coach,' declared Joe later, as they sat downstairs in the pawn shop kitchen, biting into the bread and sausage Jemima gave him from her meagre food supply. She'd divided a sausage given to her by a kindly market stallholder into three parts, one part for Joe who ate it gratefully, one for M'harty the dog, who gulped down his share then licked his lips watched her with gimlet eyes as she bit into her part, hoping for another mouthful.

Jemima didn't think the injured man's breath smelled of drink. In any case, she wasn't wondering how he fell off the coach near her doorstep, but how she could deal with him when he recovered.

As if reading her thoughts, Joe asked, 'What are you going to do with him?' He jerked his thumb towards the bedroom upstairs, as he swilled down the last of his food with the last bottle of beer that had belonged to Jemima's father, the late Mr Tom Perrot.

Jemima, thinking of her earlier attraction to this male figure, smiled mischievously.

'I think I'll keep him as a pet!'

Joe guffawed. 'Just you be careful my dear. He'll be more than you can handle when he comes round. Get a peeler to take him into custody.'

She threw her last mouthful of sausage to the dog as she chewed quickly and swallowed.

'Indeed I will not! He's done nothing wrong.'

'Oh arr, but a young buck like that is capable of making trouble I reckon, so get him out of here before he causes you to regret taking him in.'

She chuckled. 'I don't intend to remain on the shelf forever, Joe. I have little chance to meet the kind of men I would want to marry. Now fate has dropped one I fancy right outside my door. So I might keep him in the shop like an unclaimed pawned object.'

Joe roared with laughter. Then he quietened down and felt for her hand.

'Seriously, my dear, you are a kind young lady, and I've been told you are most attractive. Honour among thieves prevents anyone round here from harming you, but be careful of that young fellow upstairs. He could be a danger to an unprotected woman such as yourself.'

Young ladies were not supposed to understand what that meant, but now Jemima was surrounded by low life her recent education had taken her far beyond what her ladies' seminary had taught her.

The odd feeling that she may have seen him before came into her mind again. Yet if he was indeed a friend of her brother — or one of her father's customers she remembered seeing in his shop, what did it matter anyway?

'Of course I'll be wary of him, Joe. But he's injured — unconscious — and he'll have to stay here tonight. I'll sleep downstairs.' She smiled and continued, 'After a good night's sleep, he'll be well enough and most likely be on his way by tomorrow.' She sighed saying sorrowfully, 'And I shall be on my own again.'

Indeed, her prospects were not good — close to dire, in fact. She'd not been as able a shopkeeper as her father had been and her funds were dangerously low. Still, she anticipated that would change soon, because she'd met an old neighbour who had informed her that letters from her brother had arrived at her father's gutted shop in the Strand.

Jemima had been able to collect and read those letters and she had learned that Charles was at last on his way back to England.

In the meantime, she had to continue to scrape a living as a pawnbroker, and dress like a maid to hide her attractive female figure.

Bravely, she was making a good job of it, although she now longed whole-heartedly to return to her previous life of being a young lady.

# 3

William remembered he'd lost his balance and slid off his seat when the carriage had been violently jolted. He'd been feeling exhausted, too tired to cling on, and had toppled out of the coach onto the hard ground.

As if that wasn't enough injury, he'd then been pounced on by a gang of thieves and had been none too gently robbed!

He'd pretended to be unconscious all the time, when at times he was well aware of the young woman he heard the henchman call Jemima when she had bade him be moved. He was carried by the hefty man she called Joe into her house — and he recalled a yappy terrier Joe called M'harty.

He'd been carried upstairs and laid on a bed, where she'd tended his wounds, and then the pair had left him to recover in a bedroom.

A little later when he'd heard her say goodbye to the blind man and his dog, William braced himself against his pains and rose from the bed, anxious to escape from this den of thieves.

Looking out of the bedroom window, William could see little as it was moonlight, but he gathered he was in a poor district — somewhere near the docks.

'Damn! Now I will have missed the ship that was to have taken me out of the country!' he muttered. 'And that wretched girl and that man downstairs have taken all my cash — and my clothes and luggage have been lost.'

Struck by his bad luck, he wondered why so much harm had been heaped on him. Was there no end to it? He was faced with a dilemma.

Even in the semi darkness he guessed he was in a man's bedroom, and going to the chest of drawers he was able to find some clothes he could wear: breeches, a shirt, and a jacket that had seen better days. He found some stockings but no boots or shoes.

He was injured and half dressed, but knew he could escape from this area and walk back to his house in Mayfair. Although it would be a long, painful trudge as he tried to find his way out of the warren of streets until he got back to his familiar London territory. Also, he was afraid he might be attacked again, although there was more likelihood of being stopped by watchmen or picked up by the police because he was a fugitive.

If he were caught, it would mean prison and a hanging for him — he was being hunted by the law for murder!

Unable to find his coat or boots, he crept downstairs where he saw Jemima in the kitchen. There was the unforgettable sight of the poorly dressed but beautiful thieving miss, lying on a makeshift bed in front of the kitchen range fire.

Struck by a sudden attraction for her even in that dark kitchen, he stood wondering why — but after he'd fallen out of the carriage maybe his mind was playing tricks on him? He ought to get away from here — with all speed. Yet indeed, he longed to stay and kiss her that night!

He had a difficult choice to make. He could conceal his presence and escape her house — shoeless and penniless though he now was. If he revealed himself to her she might scream and that bruiser, Joe, might return, then William feared his body would be found floating in the Thames next morning!

William had to think of his survival first. So he decided to get out of the house — which appeared to be a shop of sorts — as soon as he was sure she'd fallen deeply asleep.

★   ★   ★

William had a very long overnight trudge in his stockinged feet to reach the fashionable district where his

London house was. Being improperly dressed, and his valuables stolen, he had to keep out of sight of anyone as much as he could.

Once in Mayfair and in front of his town house, his old butler had to be roused in the early morning and argued with. The short-sighted servant was annoyed to be woken in the early hours and did not believe, at first, that the ill-dressed and exhausted man on the doorstep was not a drunk — he was really William, the Earl of Swanington. That was partly because he believed his master had left England hours ago. William explained he'd suffered an accident on the road and missed the boat.

The accident story the butler could observe — he could also recognise the sound of the Earl's voice and his manner of speaking. Tactfully, he made no comment, but merely said, as he backed up so that his master could enter the spacious London house hall, 'A messenger came for you soon after you left for the docks, m'lord.'

His butler then offered his lordship a letter on a silver salver that had been delivered for him.

Having read the letter, William rejoiced to have received such good news! He smiled saying, 'You may tell the staff in the morning that I no longer have to depart the country. I am no longer a crime suspect for they have proved I was nowhere near the place where the maid was murdered — although they have not yet caught the culprit.'

His butler, bowed, saying, 'We never thought you were guilty, m'lord. And I'm sure we will all be glad you are free.'

Thankful to be safe and back in his home, William immediately went to bed and slumbered the clock around.

The following day, after he'd recovered, William sent for the Thames River Police to find the port's thieves who had stolen his clothes and money.

After some days the police reported back that his possessions had vanished like a sea mist. Although one dockside thief, threatened with deportation or worse, admitted that some of his things had been pawned in a dolly-shop owned by a young woman by the name of Miss Jemima Perrot.

Unfortunately, by the time the police had located Jemima's pawn shop it was several weeks later, and it was closed. The owner had flown.

However, the young earl was more interested in her, rather than what she had stolen from him, and so his search for Miss Jemima Perrot began.

★　★　★

Six months later a ball was held to start the London social season. The unmarried William Goldworthy, Earl of Swaning-ton, was considered a magnificent catch for any single lady.

He was a good-looking, confident young aristocrat, always well dressed, without appearing fussed about his looks. His wealth was known to be considerable, as was his ownership of vast swathes of the countryside. He made only an occasional appearance at social events during the London Season, and even then his lordship appeared disappointed as he assessed the year's clutch of debutantes and other unattached women. So much so that he had soon been deemed to be unobtainable by the mamas who had come hoping to find a suitable partner for their offspring.

In any case, there was that slight whiff of scandal still lingering around him. The question being rumoured around by society gossips was that his reputation had been besmirched. Some in Society were unsure whether to cut him or not.

Marriage was always a risk, but even wealth and a title did not always tempt unmarried females. There were other things to be considered. No young lady wanted to marry a gambler or a man too fond of drink or other forms of debauchery. And certainly not a murderer!

However, unknown to anyone, the handsome young earl had already chosen his bride to be — but where that beautiful sleeping beauty he remembered, that thieving miss, Jemima Perrot, was to be found was his private quest.

As he stood at the side of the ballroom, tapping his foot in time with the orchestra playing the dance tunes and watching the lady dancers trip around with their male partners, William knew it was quite illogical that he should have been smitten with attraction for a young woman like Jemima — clearly a woman from the gutter.

But was she?

He'd thought it peculiar that the glimpses he'd had of Miss Perrot's agreeable face and figure should have remained with him. It was a mystery to him. Her accent did not fit in with the normal way of speaking a dockside woman would use. Nor did her behaviour, nor her gentle tending of his wounds suggest she was a coarse type of woman. She was not at all as he would have imagined a pawn shop owner would be like. Nor was she like a thief — but then what did he know about villains? Hadn't he been recently called a villain himself?

So, on that particular evening, as the melodies from the scratchy violins provided lively dance music for the stamping men's shoes, his eyes surveyed the candlelit ballroom — and he gasped. He held his breath because among the swirling muslins and ribbons of the dancing ladies, he caught sight of a certain young lady.

There she was!

He was sure of it; Miss Jemima Perrot, the enchanting young lady of his dreams. The one woman in all of England he could not dispel from his mind. Yet he did not know why that was.

Yes, he was sure of it, even after months of searching for her. It was indeed Miss Jemima Perrot, who had stolen all he possessed that night when he'd been so exhausted from travelling for three days non-stop, being chased by the constables, and then fallen off the coach in dockland.

She'd taken all the money he'd had on him — which was significant because he'd been going abroad with a vast sum. Also, she'd taken all the valuables he had on his person — his gold watch, cufflinks, snuff box, cravat pin and ring. She'd taken everything — including his leather boots. The hussy! Then, according to the police, she had sold his belongings in her pawnshop.

No wonder he was seeing her dancing at the Duchess of Knightsbridge's ball, looking ravishing in a silk gown — made, he was sure, by a dressmaker of the highest quality, for which she would have been charged a pretty penny. His money, of course!

Even so, he could not help himself from being enthralled by her, and not just because she was so bold to be dancing the night away in the heart of Society in finery bought with his money, but because he loved the way she looked. He was amused because she behaved as if butter wouldn't melt in her mouth!

A rueful smile formed on his lips as he thought that, although he knew her to be a brazen thief she had stolen his heart too! For some absurd reason he had fallen in love with her, and seeing her again tonight had not lessened his desire. He knew that because he just couldn't bring himself to consider marrying any other female, or even to think of any other woman. Jemima was constantly on his mind.

'But now, at last, I've collared you!' he exclaimed triumphantly, ignoring all curious and scandalised eyes turned in his direction after his loud declaration.

\* \* \*

Jemima almost fainted when she noticed whose eyes were fixed on her as she danced that evening. He was the man she would always remember — the gentleman who had fallen off the coach in Gin Lane some months ago.

It was he, she felt certain, because just glancing at him brought stirrings of desire for him. Yes, he was undoubtedly the injured man she'd helped off the road and had taken to her shop. She had fancied him then — and still did.

A shiver ran though her because he seemed to be examining every inch of her.

*Perhaps he will approach me, and thank me for the help I gave him. He slipped away from the pawn shop without a work of thanks*, she thought.

'Who's that young gentleman over there staring at me?' she asked her dance partner, a military man whose red coat and trappings showed him to be a high ranked officer.

'That young buck standing by the door? He's the Earl of Swanington.'

'Did you say he is an earl?' Jemima gasped.

The officer continued, 'Yes, I recognise those noble features. I know it is him. He's a member of Whites.'

'What do you know of him?'

'Only what most people know . . . his father died years ago when he was a boy, so now that young fellow is one of the richest aristocrats in the West Country. Usually he appears uninterested in attending social occasions, yet I understand he has some good friends. Tonight, however, he looks unusually alive, as if he is hunting for a woman. You'd better watch out, ma'am, for his eyes are on you, and I understand he can be as deadly as a tarantula!'

Jemima's widened in horror. 'How so?'

'His lordship was obliged to hop abroad for a while a few weeks ago — it was said he murdered one of his servant girls.'

Jemima gave a shudder. Her throat became dry and she swallowed hard, thinking she could not believe that the man she'd taken to her home could possibly be a killer! If so, she had been most fortunate that he had run off during the night and not harmed her. She had met many rogues when she was living at Gin Lane — and none were the least like that nobleman.

She replied, 'Coming to think of it I did hear stories of a disgraced earl some time ago.'

'That was probably him. The scandal caused quite a stir.'

'Was he guilty?'

The officer shrugged. 'I don't know the ins and outs of the case. However, he ain't afraid to show his face now — and no one's objecting, so he must have been cleared of the charge. Anyway, he ain't the only man in this room to have slaughtered someone. I killed at least four of Napoleon's men at Corunna. Now, let me escort you back to your chaperone and fetch you some refreshment. I think the exertion of the dance has left you losing your voice.'

Of course, Jemima's loss of voice — and the feeling that she was about to faint — was not only hearing about the earl's reputation, for now she was worried about her own, too.

She'd managed successfully to return into Society after her brother had come home, without anyone knowing about her temporary fall into destitution. But now she had seen a man who knew where she had been only a few months ago, and she was afraid he might reveal her secret. She knew nothing about the kind of man he was, but if he'd been accused of murder, it didn't sound at all promising. He might, if he was a disreputable character, shatter hers.

'Thank you, I would like a lemonade,' Jemima managed to murmur as she sat down at the side of the dance floor in the comparative safety of a huddle of older ladies and fanned herself rapidly with the exquisite fan her brother had brought back for her from China.

She wondered how she was going to deal with the potentially disastrous situation.

Moments later it was not the

ex-soldier who brought her a glass of lemonade, but the tall and commanding Earl Swanington — attired, she noticed, in the best of fashionable men's evening wear. Quite a change from what he was wearing the last time she had seen him!

'Your drink, Miss Jemima.' His deep voice sounded as resonant as the deepest chime in the church bells and his lips twisted into a wry hint of a smile.

*Like the clanging bell of doom,* she thought, feeling as mesmerised as a rabbit confronted by a lurcher. *How dare he use my first name when we have not been properly introduced?*

The gleam in his eyes as he confronted her frightened her enough to make her want to leap up and run out of the ballroom. But making an exhibition of herself, with him possibly chasing after her, was not the best way to deal with the situation. She had to appear calm.

It would be useless to deny that she had suddenly recognised him, or that she had once dwelled in near destitution in Gin Lane. She must simply wait for him to disgrace her in front of everyone — if he intended to do that.

She accepted the proffered glass and murmured, 'Thank you, sir. My throat has become a little dry,' and took a sip of the soothing liquid.

He asked, 'May I join you?'

She gave the lightest nod and shivers crept through her as he sat next to her — the matron she had hired as chaperone, seeing the assured nobleman approaching, had vacated her seat.

William said, 'I am not surprised you've lost your voice seeing me here. The last time we met our situation was somewhat different, eh?'

Closing her eyes momentarily, Jemima wished herself a million miles away. How stupid of her to think she could appear in Society, thinking no one would find her and betray her past misfortune. However, she had done nothing wrong and he ought to be thanking her for rescuing him, not embarrassing her!

Hearing no reply from her, he continued, 'A Gin Lane address is unlike any from where everyone here resides, is it not?'

Wilting under his verbal attack she almost dropped her lemonade glass. Was he going to make a scene and reveal her time of poverty to Society?

'Poverty is no sin, my lord. It is misfortune.'

'Ah, yes, ma'am, but getting out of poverty by means of theft *is* a sin.'

Stung by his words, Jemima gave a start. Shocked that the matron's ears would be alert to hearing anything they said, she hissed, 'I agree entirely, but it was not so in my case.'

She was aware he was looking at her profile as she tried to avoid his accusing eyes by fixing her attention straight ahead at the dancers preparing for a cotillion.

He said, not as quietly as he might, 'And yet, I question if it was not so. My jewelled cravat pin and silk top hat, my tasselled hussar boots, among other things were found to be on sale in your pawn shop.'

Jemima's mind whirled. Yes, that was possible. The thieves who had stolen his valuables could have taken them to her shop to pawn them after she had left. She would not have known about it because soon after his carriage accident her brother had returned from buying goods abroad, and as he was able to provide for her she had quickly moved out. What had happened in the shop after she left she had no idea. She thought it had been closed but maybe someone else had taken it over.

Protesting in a clear, yet hushed voice, she said, 'I had nothing to do with the sale of unclaimed items. While I was there, I merely assessed items for loaning cash.' The rosy glow growing over her face embarrassed her but she felt her only defence was to be completely honest. 'I was not aware that I had pawned anything stolen.'

He gave a snort of a laugh.

She shuddered and managed another sip of her drink with a shaky hand, which enabled her to reply, 'That evening after your accident, I simply helped to move you to a place of safety after you had been robbed.' She drew in some extra breath and added clearly, 'As to who stole your personal belongings, I do not know. And who took them to the shop, I do not know. They were certainly not brought in while I was there, although it is true the shop sometimes sold unclaimed items, which pawn shops are entitled to do.'

'Ah, but how did my valuables come to be in your shop in the first place? My gold watch belonged to my father — sentimental of me to want it back, you may say, but robbers, in their greed, rarely think of the harm they do.'

'I agree. I have experienced losing my treasured things. Not stolen, but lost all the same.'

He had no reply to that.

Jemima thought it best to continue being truthful. 'I tell you that I was not aware of handling anything of yours, although we had a great many gentlemen's items brought in to be pawned.'

'Mostly stolen, eh?'

Fanning her face vigorously to hide her annoyance, she replied, 'Some items may have been, but my intention was to assist men and women who desperately needed money and had to pawn their own valuables.'

His eyes narrowed as he leant over to whisper, 'But you did well out of it by the display of finery on you now.'

How could he be so crass, so certain he was right that he did not mind saying things that would embarrass her in the midst of a group of ladies whose eyes and ears must be enjoying seeing the two of them verbally sparing — even if they did not understand what they were talking about.

Jemima took a deep breath, then protested, 'Not so, my lord. I managed to survive after my father lost all his wealth, and we ran the pawn broker's business. But then my brother came home from China and and now has been able to provide me a generous allowance.'

He gave a mocking laugh. 'A

convenient story. A brother appearing like a fairy godfather!'

She would have dropped her glass if his hand had not shot out and taken it from her.

'Nevertheless, it is true,' she managed to say. 'I do have a kind brother. He was abroad when the tragedy occurred and my papa died, but now he is returned he is busy building up my father's lost trade in Chinese goods — that is why he is not here tonight. He has little taste for entertainments, but he is keen for me to resume my place in Society.' Jemima felt she might as well stick to the truth, so she added, 'And for me to seek a suitable husband.'

'Am I being asked to believe that?'

She bristled, 'Some people find me attractive, my lord, even if you do not!'

He smiled and lowering his eyes, scanned her figure as she sat upright in her chair.

'Oh, I did not say you are not desirable, Miss Perrot. Indeed, you attract me very much.'

Heavens! Whatever would he say next?

Blushing behind her hastily spread fan, Jemima said, 'This is hardly the place to discuss such matters, my lord.'

'Very well,' he agreed, twirling the contents of his glass in his long fingers, and throwing back his head drank it all. She doubted it was lemonade. He beamed at her and suggested, 'Shall I escort you outside into the garden?'

She did not like the sound of that. Being alone with a man was not considered at all proper for an unmarried lady. But would he threaten her if she did not leave with him? Or was it a good opportunity to straighten out the misunderstanding he had about her?

She fanned her hot face vigorously. Turning, she bravely looked at the countenance of a man whom she could not believe would harm her saying, 'How will I know if you just want an opportunity to . . . to murder me? For that is what I hear you have been accused of, is it not?'

The quick change of his expression

made her realise she was not the only one feeling vulnerable. His frown made it clear to her that he had an unfortunate time in his past life he wanted to conceal too. She realised that being classified as a criminal — even if only temporarily — had been most unpleasant for him.

She had heard about his orphaned childhood too. Rich, he might be, but not blessed in other ways it seemed.

However, he immediately took control of the situation and lowered his head to whisper in her ear, 'Let us be civilised, Miss Perrot. A stroll outside in the garden away from all the listening ears around us, may be a little chilly for you in your décolleté ball gown, but it will give us privacy to talk and — '

'And give you the opportunity to ravish me!' she hissed, snapping her fan closed sharply.

He chuckled softly. 'Only if you wish it!'

In spite of herself, she had to smile at his audacity.

He would know she could not have resided in Gin Lane and been unaware of the low life there and would understand the dangers women faced. But she coloured deeper knowing her daydreams about him were not entirely innocent, and after meeting him again her admiration for his fine-looking face and figure had reinforced her desire for him to kiss her.

Knowing that they both needed to overcome painful events in their past, made them partners in a curious way.

'Perhaps a little fresh air might do us good,' she said, standing and slipping her gloved hand into the arm he offered her.

Everyone could see them walking gracefully together out of the ballroom — but they could not hear her heart beating a wild dance.

# 4

The moonlit garden and sharp breeze would have made Jemima feel cold if she did not already feel warm all over with embarrassment.

An owl's call replaced the sound of the dance orchestra after they had stepped out of the French windows and strolled further away from the music in the extensive garden. Soon they were surrounded by exotic imported trees, perfumed shrubs, and colourful flower beds.

How the red geraniums glowed in the evening light — like her complexion, Jemima feared.

When the candlelit ballroom was left far behind them Jemima noticed his firm hand holding her arm. At first they did not talk, it seemed right for her to be escorted by him far away from listening ears and she noted the looks of incredulity they had received from female dancers and matrons.

Jemima had been aware that everyone who saw them together could not hide their curiosity at seeing the Earl of Swanington had chosen a lady at last! Was it envious looks Jemima noticed them give her? Or were they amazed that she would consent to accompany that tainted aristocrat outside without her chaperone?

She asked herself why was it that she was not afraid of him. He was well-mannered, but a muscular man — she had seen him in a state of near undress and she had not been able to forget him. She had to admit that if she had ever hoped to meet her Prince Charming, it was him!

Used to dealing with male customers that came into her shop, she was unlike the unmarried young women dancing in the ballroom, whose experience of men was yet to come. Jemima was not afraid to argue and defend her position. But she could not ignore his taunts about her honesty. She wanted to set matters straight, at least try to explain and get rid of his accusation that she was a thief.

How could she hope to marry anyone if this nobleman was to betray her secret and expose her as a thief as he thought she was?

She felt angry too. Had she not suffered enough when disaster had struck her father, and worked hard to overcome it? Now she wanted to put the humiliation of being destitute out of her mind. Society had welcomed her as if she had never been out of it — until he had suddenly turned up to spoil things.

Well out of sight and sound of the ballroom, in the middle of a lawn where no one could overhear them talking, William stopped walking and, turning to her, he said, 'Now, what makes you think I would want murder you?'

'What makes you think I am a thief?'

'Hmm. I see we need to be frank with each other, do we not? Shall we start with a kiss — for you look very desirable to me.'

She was shocked by his suggestion — did he think living in Gin Lane had made her into a harlot?

But was not a kiss exactly what she had often secretly hoped would happen between them! At twenty-six years of age she wanted a taste of love before she became too old and stuck on the shelf.

She managed to keep her voice level as she replied, 'I am sure the pleasure for you would be greater than it would for me, my lord.'

'How so? I understand women enjoy being kissed.'

She suspected by the gleam in his eye that he was teasing her, but at that moment she said truthfully, 'I think women like to know who they are kissing. I suspect you know more about me than I know about you.'

'I know very little about you except your name is Miss Jemima Perrot.' He straightened his back and looked down at her, showing the arrogance of his pedigree. 'I am sure you know who I am.'

Jemima lifted her eyes to meet his challenging expression. 'I learned only this evening from my dance partner that you are the Earl of Swanington.'

He bowed, obliging her to curtsy.

'Now we are properly introduced,' he said, giving her a charming smile that made her knees feel weak, 'Please, call me William.'

For some reason she remembered the story she had heard as a child about Little Red Riding Hood and the crafty fox. There was something decidedly foxy about the way he was treating her!

He was reported to have had a criminal record. A murderer, no less! Looking at him there was no way she could tell if he was indeed a villain.

But why did she not feel afraid of him? Because there was something about him that made her feel safe — now was that not strange?

★  ★  ★

William did not like to say that meeting her again dressed so fashionably and beautifully was a delightful treat in itself. It reinforced his first encounter with her — that instant attraction and desire to make love to her. But the circumstances of their meetings were unusual. He could not show her those feelings the first time they had seen each other that night in the Strand watching the fire, or in the dockland — and he could not now. It was not that he did not want to kiss her, looking so beautiful in her ball gown with her dressed hair, of course he did. But primarily, he had to straighten out the misunderstandings between them, learn why she denied robbing him, and why she seemed to live a double life — in poverty one minute, and in Society the next.

Very peculiar! Fascinating, too. Her background intrigued him much more than any other pretty young innocent.

He also needed to explain his unfortunate involvement in the murder of his housemaid — and that business was better done before thinking about satisfying his lust!

As they continued to stroll through the long grass in the moonlight, Jemima thought she owed him an explanation, and began to explain why her father owned a pawn shop.

'I want you to understand that my father was ruined by a kitchen fire that the servants were unable to contain. Quite suddenly the flames licked through the building and in no time it had destroyed his fashionable fan shop — and our home and everything in it.'

The memory of the disaster brought tears into her eyes. She looked up through her tears and saw he was listening with a grim, but not unsympathetic expression, so she continued.

'Papa, was mentally injured by the disaster too. He needed to continue being a shopkeeper as he had always been since he was a boy. He took great pride in his work as a shopkeeper of Chinoiserie. Chinese goods are very fashionable and he had built up a good trade and reputation. Even the Prince of Wales was one of his customers.'

She drew in a long breath, then releasing it went on, 'After the disaster, we could have relied on friends to support us but my father wanted to be independent. Taking on the pawn shop — even in a poor district — gave him some sense of respectability. He was not a pauper, but an honest man, sir. You, as an aristocrat with wealth, may not understand that many ordinary men take great pride in their occupation, skills they have learned over the years. Men, and some women too, love their chosen way of life.'

'Is that why you were in that poor district?'

'Indeed it was. I loved my papa and wanted to look after him. And while I was there I learned the pawn trade — in fact, I found it very interesting. Meeting good people you would regard as low class, people I would never have met as a fashionable young lady. The experience gave me a greater under-standing of how other people live, of their joys and sorrows.'

'How did you manage to make a deal of money from the pawnshop?'

Aware that he was assessing her fashionable gown she replied, 'We did not. We only managed to scrape a meagre living. My father always ran a fair, honest business, helping those in debt if he could, and I endeavoured to do the same, which was not always easy in the area of London where crime was rife.'

Seeing she had his attention and was not interrupting, Jemima continued, 'My present wealth is due to my kind brother, as I have explained, who returned from abroad and has been busy recover-ing our fortunes.'

He nodded as if accepting her story was true.

'I do not deny that I was destitute for a while. I had to behave as any other working woman — roll my sleeves up and wash, cook and clean in the poor circumstances I was in — but in no way do I regret the experience. People are good and bad in all levels of society and I certainly met many good people as well as rogues in the Dockland.'

She was surprised to see he nodded again. He was an earl — what did he know of the underworld? Then she remembered that he probably did. Like her, he had recently been cast out of Society.

Jemima went on to tell of her father's illness and demise, which had left her to continue the pawnbroker's work of taking something valuable from someone for lending cash, which she assured him she did with integrity.

Finally, she told of her brother Charles and of his recent return from China, and her good living being restored — except, of course, she was now no longer a woman without experience of life.

Jemima, almost breathless in her haste to exonerate herself, finished her account to explain her past and present situations. She was gratified to see the earl had patiently listened to her story.

She now waited to hear his account of himself.

★ ★ ★

William wanted to believe her explanation as she sounded sincere and he could think of no reason why she was not telling him the truth, outlandish as it was.

They stood looking for some time at each other and she seemed to be waiting for his response.

After the silence he cleared his throat and said, 'I respect your courage, ma'am. My life too was turned upside down when I was hiding from those who accused me of murder. It is not easy sometimes to make people believe the truth when things appear the opposite.'

Now there was a definite link between them, a growing understanding because of misfortune which had overtaken them both in different ways. When she looked up at him and smiled,

71

he automatically turned his head to smile down at her. Their eyes stayed locked and for a while, they said no more.

Jemima did not object when he drew her gently into his arms, for her wish to feel his desire for her was as strong as hers was for him. Their kiss was as natural as the darkness of the night.

They had revealed something of themselves. Whether they were both being absolutely truthful neither of them knew, but they had discovered enough to want to get to know each other better.

As it was chilly they walked on in silence until they came across an ornamental fountain, its playing water like soft music. Pausing, they both stared at the female figurine afloat on a shell surrounded by the fish spraying jets of water splashing gently over her. It made William think of the shapely woman beside him — but he must talk to her first.

'Let me explain my situation now,' he said, sitting on the edge of the fountain and leaning over to play his long fingers across the water's surface. 'Early in the new year, a maid in my country household was found with her throat cut, unmistakably murdered.'

Hearing that bold statement, Jemima gasped.

'I was accused of the crime.'

He studied her face noting her horror. He turned to look at the cascading water and remarked, 'Of course, living where you were, you will be accustomed to hearing about cut-throats.'

Trying to remain calm, she retorted, 'Crimes can be committed anywhere, my lord.'

He nodded. Seeing her looking around uneasily, he went on, 'Be not afraid. I may be guilty of many things but I have never killed anyone.'

Jemima thought deeply as she listened to him intently, wanting to trust this man she was so attracted to. Was he a rake? Had he a penchant for pretty maids and had met one who had refused him — and in a struggle with her had killed her, even accidentally? Yet, why would he have a knife on him to kill her in such a grievous way unless the crime was premeditated? Had the girl threatened to say that he had ravished her?

While Jemima was trying to sort out her troubled mind, he went on, 'I was nowhere near the mill where she was murdered that night, although some people said I was.'

'Where were you?'

'Away from my country house. At first I had difficultly proving I was in Plymouth. The weather had been good and the sea mild, so I had agreed to sail my boat there with a man on my estate whose young son wanted to join the Navy. I was providing the thirteen-year-old boy with some experience of life on board ship before he finally made up his mind to leave his family, and the captain of the ship *Endeavour* took him on as a midshipman.'

That, thought Jemima, was a kind thing for him to have done.

William went on to explain, 'Unfortunately, after I sailed back home with the boy's father, I found there was a hue and cry after me. I was being hunted by officers of the law who had been falsely told I had murdered the maid.'

Jemima had heard of people in Dockland hiding from the Thames police, who had been accused of crimes they had not been guilty of. It was certainly possible that what she was being told was the truth, especially if he had witnesses that could prove he was nowhere near the scene of the crime at the time. But the earl was a rich man — he could easily have bribed some people to say he was elsewhere.

Her doubting expression made him pause and look away from her. He brushed his fingers through his hair in exasperation.

'My problem is that the murderer has not been caught and while he — or she — is free, I will always be under some suspicion.'

At last she did sympathise with his

position, but could think of nothing to say to ease his suffering, for she felt sure he was still feeling the weight of it.

He turned to look at her and she saw his eyes glisten with tears. He was, she felt sure, telling the truth but he had this awful curse on him as he said, 'I can understand your unease to be with me, Jemima. My reputation has been ruined. My word is no longer to be taken as the truth.'

Was she to trust him? This was something different from the strong feeling of physical attraction she felt for him.

Guessing she was still making up her mind he went on, 'Let me confess that I was terrified after being accused of murder. I hid for a while — my grandmother helped me — and I made arrangements to emigrate.

'I was making a dash abroad when I fell off the coach near your shop and my things were snatched. This prevented me from sailing. Yet it turned out to be fortuitous because I learned when I returned to my townhouse that my name had been cleared. The Captain of the *Endeavour* had sent word to confirm that I was indeed in Plymouth, and evidence had been found that someone else must have killed the girl.' He gave a great sigh. 'However, because the murderer has not been caught, I am trying to discover who it is. The investigation is taking up all of my time but I am frustrated at having no success at it.'

She made no comment, so he went on, 'I am a young man with a desire to run my estates responsibly. I wish to be married, not spend the rest of my life chasing shadows. Whoever did me harm by accusing me of murder, is preventing me from living a normal life. I must find the guilty person before they do me more evil.'

Finding her voice, Jemima asked, 'I am sure you have the search in hand?'

'Yes, indeed. But please understand that it was not easy for me to contact witnesses who proved that I had spent the evening elsewhere and was not at my country house at the time when the murder was committed, not when some were saying I was guilty. My planned flight from England was because I was in a panic and feared I might be lynched without a proper trial.'

She could appreciate that he would be afraid of such, as indeed so would she in his position. She said, 'I asked you to believe what happened to me — and so I must also believe you.'

Sitting down in front of him on the low stone wall surrounding the fountain, seemingly unaware that the jets of cold water were showering her lightly, the aura of haze enhanced her figure and her hair sparkled with the droplets of water, making her appear angelic.

Remembering how she had come to his aid when he was unconscious and had helped him to shelter with the aid of blind Joe, he began to realise she could indeed be an angel — instead of a thief as he had previously suspected! The change in his mind about her made him clear his throat.

'Your transformation from looking like a dockland maid to the elegant lady I see before me is remarkable. Your silk gown suits you admirably, and your manners suggest you really are a young woman who has suffered grievously and overcome great misfortune.'

She replied, 'I know you are trying to accept that what I have told you is the truth, just as you are expecting me to believe your story. My beautiful gown and jewels do not come from my selling your belongings, my lord. I repeat, whatever was stolen from you was taken by thieves in Gin Lane. I swear I have no idea what happened to them. I ran an honest pawnbroking business, taking it over from my father. Please understand that after my beloved papa died I had no other means of support — until my brother Charles returned from China. You may check my explanation if you wish.'

She turned her eyes to study his. Human beings could affect each other, but even so, they knew so little of what went on in another person's head. Although they had revealed their secrets to each other, this handsome nobleman before her was still a stranger — a man about whom she still had so much to learn.

At last he showed he seemed to have accepted her explanation by saying, 'If that is indeed the case, Miss Perrot, then I owe you an apology — and many thanks. Now, how shall I repay you?'

They looked deeply into each other's eyes as water droplets sprayed them and seemed to wash away the misunderstanding between them.

His offer seemed sincere, so she replied, 'I ask for no repayment for what was an act of mercy. You needed help and I did my best. I had no money at that time to hire a carriage to send you home — I did not know where you lived in any case, nor who you were.'

'Well, you know now, and I am prepared to offer you a great deal as a reward.'

Jemima felt sure he meant it, although she replied, 'I assure you, there is nothing I need, my lord. My brother gives me a very generous allowance. I only ask one thing . . . I beg you do not betray my time of misfortune to High Society. Many like to tittle-tattle, and would be enthralled by a story of rags to riches like mine, ruining my reputation — and chance of matrimony. Some would undoubtedly enjoy hearing about my humiliation and — '

'Not I, nor any other true gentleman, I assure you! I get no pleasure from harming others.' After agreeing not to make her time of penury known, and accepting his awkward position of being accused of a crime, he stated, 'We have agreed to believe and trust each other, have we not?'

If it was difficult for her to believe his explanation, difficult for her to trust him, was it not just as hard for him to believe her too? She had to decide.

She took a deep breath and said, 'Yes, my lord, I think we can agree on that.'

Patting her damp hair, she looked searchingly into his eyes and thought how beautifully sapphire-coloured they were. She continued looking at him for a long time as he appeared to be content to study her. She longed for him to kiss her, but now that she knew he was way above her in rank, she feared being his mistress would be the closest she could ever be to him. She did not want that.

She felt greatly relieved when he smiled at her warmly, taking her hand gently and kissing it.

'Then it is a bargain between us. I assure you I would take no pleasure from ruining your future or indeed harming you in any way.'

She had to trust him or worry all her life that he might not keep his word. Now was the time to say goodbye. He to continue with his life, living like a lord, and she, living a spinster's existence.

Fate had brought them together when he had come into her life by accident, toppled off a carriage at her feet!

She recognised he was someone special; a man she was anxious not to be parted from, of whom she longed to know more.

He was a nobleman in his air and bearing, had been nothing other than polite, even though he accused her of theft — which was understandable — but now that the matter had been explained they could get to know each other better, and she desired that.

'As we are revealing ourselves and you have told me about your virtues, perhaps you will confess your wayward ways?'

He gave a laugh. 'No indeed I will not! You will find them out soon enough.'

Fascinated by his challenging remark she asked, 'How so? We may not meet again, as you are unlikely to visit our new Chinese shop looking to buy a fan.'

'We might make our relationship a little closer.'

His meaning was made clear in his pleading eyes, his hushed voice. Jemima's body ached for his caresses.

They rose and she moved close, looking up at him quite boldly and saying, 'I too admit to having some faults, William, but I always try to be truthful.'

He seemed amazed at first that she seemed to be asking to be kissed. But then, he knew she was no innocent maid coming out into Society.

He studied her, absorbed, as his long-figured hand gently stroked her damp hair, and the side of her soft face, before he bent and placed his lips lightly on hers. A wave of excitement and pleasure crashed over her and left her breathless, enraptured by a passion she had not even dreamed of, but she revelled in it.

He eased her away saying, 'One finer side of my character is that I do not ravish women.'

Jemima came down to earth painfully.

Had she been too forward? Much as she had enjoyed his gentle kisses it was a dangerous game she was playing. How could she be so stupid, so wanton?

'Are you . . . are you tied to another lady?' she stammered, stepping away from him.

'No, I am not. Are you perhaps considering taking another gentleman's hand in marriage?'

She chuckled. 'The only male friend I have is blind Joe, and he is married and has his little dog, M'harty, whom he loves much more than I.'

He chuckled and astounded her by asking, 'Then who shall I ask for permission for your hand in marriage?'

Marriage? To him — an Earl of the Realm? Was he funning with her?

She replied a little bitterly, having tasted him and wanting more, yet knowing he was out of bounds for her, 'As an earl you have plenty of choice. My father, bless him, would have fainted if he were alive and you came to him and asked for my hand.'

He did not reply but as he came to kiss her again Jemima felt cross with herself — and him.

Suddenly she came down to earth. Heavily. Her pulse raced and she was hot with shame to have let herself be kissed by a stranger, and unchaperoned! True, she liked him and perhaps, in her imagination she thought she loved him, but he would never marry the likes of her! She was little more than a shop girl. She should not even think that that he, an earl of high standing, would seriously consider her as his marriage partner — especially after her sojourn in Gin Lane.

She had to conquer her weak impulses to enjoy his embraces and to get away from the danger he posed straight away. Impulsively, before he could stop her, she was up on her toes and her dance slippers were racing off towards the ballroom.

★ ★ ★

William did not attempt to race after her. He sat down on the side of the fountain, feeling disappointed that he had somehow upset her, and watched her pretty figure trip away and eventually disappear from sight.

Then he sighed with a smile on his face as he swirled his hand in the water. He felt sure Jemima was the woman he loved and wanted for his wife. She had shown resilience and a bold spirit which he admired in a woman. Natural beauty too, without decking herself out with the artificial aids used by many women in Society. She was willing to kiss him — perhaps even for him to make love to her. But more than that, deep down she had given him solace and he felt they were intended for each other.

He was indebted to her for saving him after being attacked that night after he had fallen off the coach and now she asked for nothing more than he should not reveal her misfortune. But he wanted to give her more, wanted to make her his countess, and to give her all his love and anything he could to make her happy.

His recent unfortunate experiences had helped him to understand the world outside of his privileged birth and upbringing. Jemima was a lady who had suffered, and although it had in no way made her less desirable he could not expect her to fall at his feet, even though many of the young ladies of Society might do so.

He should not have expected her to accept him. His grandmother would probably have said he had no right to even ask her under the circumstances. Then he thought, how would he know what his grandmother thought about Jemima, unless she'd met her? He should arrange for them to meet, for time to court Jemima properly.

After sitting for a while mulling over how good their lives might be together, William suddenly realised things were not so good.

He had let Jemima slip away and knew no more than Prince Charming did about Cinderella! He was sure she would have collected her chaperone and fled the ball by now, and he had not even a glass slipper to help him search for her.

Slapping the fountain water fiercely, he drenched himself. The shock of the cold water brought the high standing earl down to earth, as he realised he had some hunting to do.

His title and wealth had come to him by accident of birth — but his future happiness with the woman he loved, he would have to strive for in order to win her love.

# 5

M'harty was the kind of little dog that enjoyed sniffing what were for him delectable smells. Blind Joe — if he could see — would of course have dragged him away from most of what his dog found in Gin Lane, or anywhere on the streets in the poorest parts of London.

Another characteristic of M'harty was that, once he smelled someone, he never forgot them.

The Earl of Swanington was annoyed to find a perky black and white terrier yapping at his heels, as the animal began to follow him along the streets of Dockland. His lordship had been pounding the pavements for days looking for clues of where Miss Jemima Perrot might be found.

Suddenly his spirits lifted as he realised this little dog was not only friendly, but could be the blind man's dog, M'harty. Seeing a pie man, William hailed him and bought a meat pie, then placed a few scraps of the meat on the pavement and waited.

M'harty sat down and, cocking his small head on one side, licked his lips, clearly wondering if the offering was for him. He looked up at the tall man and when William said, 'It's for you to eat, M'Harty,' the dog got up, wagged his tail happily as he came trotting closer, and gobbled up the pieces of pie with relish. Then he licked his lips in anticipation of more to come.

The earl was happy to feed him. It was a new experience for William. The simple pleasures of life, like feeding animals, he had always left to his servants. Now he realised there were enjoyments in life that his lofty position had barred him from. When the dog was satisfied that the meal was at an end, he trotted off with the earl striding behind him. William was in luck to find a small back yard, where M'harty had slipped in through a broken fence. Going around to the front of the dilapidated abode he knocked on the front door.

'Yes?' A wary-looking middle-aged woman was drying her hands on her apron as she answered the door. She looked the well-dressed gentleman up and down and said defensively, 'I'll have you know we paid the rent last week.'

'I do not collect rent, ma'am. I came to speak with Joe,' said the Earl of Swanington politely, removing his hat.

A proud nobleman would not always treat a poor woman with the respect he was showing her but William was learning to adapt his lordly ways. Being naturally aloof, even sometimes appearing rudely commanding while dressed in the height of fashion, he was used to dealing with servants. But during his recent fall from grace — and his dependence on his loyal servants to hide him from the law — he had discovered that being lordly with them was not the best way to deal with ordinary people he wanted to talk with.

The woman said, 'He ain't here, sir. He be down the road with a load of ruffians in the Ship Inn, most likely.'

William asked courteously, 'Then may I wait for him to return? Mrs . . . ?'

She looked taken aback to be asked her name, but answered, 'Bundy.'

The young earl smiled at her and was delighted to see she smiled a little. 'Mrs Bundy, are you, by any chance, Joe Bundy's wife?'

She replied suspiciously, 'I am, sir.'

William's genuine beam of success made Mrs Bundy back into her house, and she would have closed the door if William had not said, loudly and clearly, 'Ma'am wait, please. I wish to give Joe some money for saving my life.'

Suspiciously, eyes almost popping out of her head, she asked, 'What was that you said?'

'I wish to repay Joe for his kindness to me.'

Clearly suspicious, Mrs Bundy almost

closed the door again, then on second thoughts, opened it and asked, 'How much, sir?'

The earl stated the huge sum, making the woman grasp and hold the door jamb for support.

William explained how Joe had carried him off the street after he had been robbed, and it eased her suspicion of him. The earl's charming manner enquiring about the housewife's blind husband's welfare as he gave her a heavy purse of much-needed sovereigns, soon gave him access into the house — as well as a cup of tea.

Mrs Bundy explained, 'Joe won't be back for hours, sir. I get his dinner ready, then his dog goes to find him and guides him home.'

William did not fancy walking into an inn full of ruffians to find Joe and speak with him.

'Mrs Bundy, I would like to know if you can tell me where I might find Miss Jemima Perrot, as I wish to reward her too.'

So with M'Harty being stroked as he sat on the nobleman's lap, William learned the full story from Mrs Bundy of how the young Miss Jemima Perrot, who dressed herself like a maid on the Dockland streets, had helped her stricken father and ran their pawn shop, until her brother returned from China a rich man, and she moved away.

'Jemima's not a hoity-toity young lady, sir. She still comes around now and again and has a cup of tea and a chat with us.'

William was ecstatic when Mrs Bundy gave him Jemima's new address and he left the house rejoicing. He could hardly wait to pay a call on Jemima now he had found out where she lived.

★ ★ ★

Jemima had been feeling unsettled for weeks after she'd met William. Now living in a stylish London house with her brother, she had adapted to her new life as a lady of leisure since Charles had returned. The initial enjoyment of seeing her brother safe and sound, and the security he was able to bring her, was wearing off. Contacting her old friends was pleasant, but except for Sylvia, they did not know about her misfortune, and Jemima did not find she shared their light-hearted interests any longer. She could not bring herself to sew, play the pianoforte, or to go shopping, nor even read a book for long — because her thoughts constantly turned to the nobleman she had lost.

Not that she thought he meant it when he offered her marriage — no, indeed, that was said only in jest — but nevertheless, she wondered about it. She did not think he was being deliberately unkind, but the more she thought about him, the more she came to the conclusion that William was exactly the kind of man she was looking to marry — but he was too high in rank for her, ending any hopes and longings she had about the matter. She would have to settle for a dull gentleman who asked for her hand, or remain a maiden aunt when Charles married.

In some ways she wished she was still busy in the pawn shop as idleness did not suit her.

If only she could get William out of her mind.

One morning as she stared unseeingly out of the parlour window not able to concentrate on anything, she blinked several times and began to perspire, because she saw his familiar figure walking up the drive, attired in the best gentleman's morning clothes.

*How on earth did he did find me? There is more to this young nobleman than I had thought!*

Hearing the parlour maid answering the door knocker's rapping, Jemima almost panicked.

*But do I really need to pretend I'm not at home? I like him and I'm thrilled to see him — although I shall not tell him that!*

Rosy-faced Peggy appeared at the

parlour door in her attractive maid's dress, bobbed and announced, 'There's ever such a 'ansome man come calling, Miss. Says he's an Earl of som'at or other. Do you want me to show him in 'ere?'

Flustered, Jemima wrung her hands together and answered, 'Yes,' then, 'No!'

She had no time to make up her mind, as the tall gentleman eased the maid aside and strode into the room with a friendly smile that made Jemima feel like melting ice.

'I should be obliged if your maid would fetch some refreshment, Miss Perrot,' he said, after bowing politely and taking off his gloves which he placed in his top hat and handed to a very surprised Peggy. 'I've been walking around all the morning, looking for your house, have had no luncheon, and feel quite fatigued.'

Jemima gave him a polite curtsy, pleased she was wearing one of her most flattering morning gowns and her hair well dressed.

He complimented her on her looks. Reassured by his easy grace and manners, Jemima sank down on a chair, and asked rather stupidly, 'Have you no carriage?'

'Several.' He winked at her. 'But I have a tendency to fall out of them!'

Peggy giggled and Jemima could not help but smile too. Yet her awe at his presence and a concern for being found out soon passed by Jemima, and she dismissed the maid, telling her to bring tea and sandwiches for his lordship.

Flummoxed at being with the man who had caused her heart no peace for months, but not knowing quite what to say to him now he had turned up unexpectedly, she began by explaining, 'My lord, please forgive my maid. She is not fully trained, nor indeed are the rest of my staff because I collected them from the gutter. They were desperate people needing a livelihood, and a chance for a better start in life. That maid might well have become a harlot, had I not helped her.'

Such a bold description from the lips of a lady would, in polite society, have caused a scandal but Jemima and William were on different terms. And William was pleased that Jemima had not put on airs and graces since her return to her position as being a lady of leisure.

He said sincerely. 'That does not surprise me. I would say it is very typical of you, Miss Perrot, to want to help others — as you did me. I admire you greatly for it.'

He made himself at home, finding a chair, flicking his coat tails behind him before he sat down, even though she had not asked him to be seated.

'I have come with a request for another favour from you — one of the most respectable kind.'

'Oh, indeed?' She knew she was shaking and her face burned, but thanks to her brother settling on her a very generous allowance she knew she had a fine house to be proud of. She was in a position to ignore anything the noble lord might propose, if she so chose.

Jemima had always managed by herself but now with no work to do, she knew her life had become somewhat pointless. Working in the pawn shop in the Docklands was far more interesting! But what William had in mind sounded intriguing, and she badly needed a more active, interesting life.

She could not ignore his warm smile, lifting the corners of his mouth. It was so enticing. It brought on the desire for him to kiss her again and she blushed to think of her need for him. At least he didn't know what she was thinking!

'Yes,' she heard him say, 'I wish to offer you a challenge — and to possibly change your life.'

She blinked, suddenly alarmed of how he could alter her circumstances.

'I trust you do not have it in mind to humiliate me?' she whispered, 'To prevent me from keeping my place in society?'

William's head perked up like a cockerel's.

'Now why ever should I want to do that?'

'Because you know of my unfortunate past.'

'Indeed I do, as you know mine. We have already discussed all that.'

She waited, hoping he was not cross. Half afraid of what he'd come to suggest. She clasped her hands tightly together and looked searchingly into his eyes.

He returned her examination for a while and then said, 'I had a long talk with Blind Joe's good lady earlier this morning. It was most informative. They told me all about your hard life in Gin Lane.'

Jemima sighed. So he had been checking on the truth of what she had told him.

She found it difficult to concentrate on his words as she was assessing his beautifully combed hairstyle, his soft lips and the fine work his valet had done to turn out a perfectly attired gentleman. Her longing for him was not diminished by the possibility of him ruining her future. No indeed, his very presence was making her body tingle all over.

Her face flushed at the thought of being held in his arms again, of kissing him as they had done only last month.

Jemima came out of her reverie as she heard him say, 'I am full of admiration for your courage and resourcefulness, Jemima, in overcoming the tragedies in your life.'

'Yes, indeed it was at times a hard and difficult experience, not living for a while like the young lady I was brought up to be,' she admitted. 'My acquaintances, my school friends, I feel sure, would not have been able to work in a pawn shop. I think they would not have survived life in Gin Lane even for a few hours!'

Jemima suddenly bubbled with laughter at the thought of her more prim friends wearing maid's clothing and arguing with customers about the price to pay them for pawning a pair of men's trousers — especially remembering some of the disreputable characters she had dealt with. But her merriment evaporated as she watched the earl seated opposite her get up and move his chair nearer to hers.

Transfixed, because she knew it was improper of him to do so, yet enjoying his company, she felt unable to protest.

'Well, Jemima,' he said, taking her hand, which sent delightful shivers along her arm and travelled to her toes. 'Those correct young ladies you describe do not interest me one jot. I wish for a lady of true spirit.'

'Where do you hope to find this lady, my lord?'

He put his fingers under her chin and moved her face towards his.

'I have been searching for some time for the right lady — and I have found her, right here,' he replied, leaning forward and surprising her by kissing her lightly.

Shocked by his forward behaviour yet

thrilled to feel the tenderness of his lips, she relished the sensation of these delicious feelings releasing her pent-up desire and she kissed him back.

Realising her need for him was growing by the minute, Jemima eased herself away, saying, 'Your search may be over, but not mine.'

She rose quickly, swept over towards the window and looked out.

He followed her, placing his large hands gently on her shoulders. It was comforting as he leaned over to whisper in her ear, 'What is it you want, Jemima?' His head lowered so that his cheek touched hers. 'Apart from me?'

He'd guessed her thoughts and she was thankful he was standing behind her and could not see her blush. How could she say that she knew their relationship could have no future? How could she accept any agreement with him except being his mistress for a while until he found the paragon of virtue he was really looking for?

A crash at the door made them part.

The door opened and the little maid rolled in a trolley with a teapot and cups and saucers wobbling on it.

Jemima smiled kindly, saying softly to her, 'A maid should be as quiet as possible, Peggy.'

'Sorry, miss.'

'Wheel the trolley over here, will you? I see you have made sandwiches.'

Jemima could see hunks of bread not as finely cut as a maid should have made. However, she did not have to apologise as William had already shown his appreciation by taking one and starting to eat it with relish.

Jemima, seeing he was hungry, said, 'I expect his lordship would like a piece of the cake the cook made this morning, too.'

'I brought it!' said Peggy proudly pointing to the fruit cake on the bottom layer of the trolley.

'But where are the cake plates?'

'You can use your sandwich plate, can't you?'

The earl assured her that would be a

good idea, and Peggy seemed relieved. Then the girl explained, 'But I didn't know where the coffee pot was, so I put the coffee in the teapot.'

Fortunately, William was amused and laughed loudly, and both Jemima and her maid joined in.

'That will do nicely, thank you, Peggy,' Jemima said as she settled down after the merriment. 'Now, you have the afternoon off, do you not?'

'Yes Miss, in the normal way I 'ave. But all the staff have left the house with things they had to do today, so I said I would stay 'ere and look after you while they was gone.'

Jemima wished to be alone with William. They had something private to discuss, she wanted to know what he had in mind, but did not want anyone around. But then she had an idea.

'I believe your sister has just had a baby and I am sure you would love to go home and see the child, would you not?'

The maid nodded eagerly. 'Yes, I'm

looking forward to seeing the baby, Miss.'

'Well then, off you go. This gentleman and I will manage to serve ourselves with coffee.'

Peggy, not knowing any better, that Jemima's proposal to be left alone with a man was not what a lady should do, readily agreed. With many joyful expressions of thanks, the maid bobbed and rushed out of the room, and soon afterwards they heard the kitchen door slam behind her.

'That was rash of you,' William remarked. 'Allowing yourself to be quite alone with me.'

Jemima hoped she had not been too impulsive and foolish as she poured the coffee and handed him a cup — which rocked slightly in her hand.

'I have frequently been alone,' she remarked somewhat sadly.

He drank the coffee thirstily, then stood up and strode across the room to look out of the window. 'I presume Peggy lives in Gin Lane?'

'Nearby.'

'There and back will take her a few hours?'

'Yes,' she whispered, knowing it was unnecessary to speak in a low voice because she knew the house was now empty of servants.

She had deliberately allowed herself to be at this nobleman's mercy just as he had been when she had found him on the Dockland streets and had taken him to her house. Her vulnerability felt dangerous but also deliciously exciting!

'Jemima,' he said, with his back to her, 'You have shown you trust me, and I am honoured.'

'It is I who feel honoured, my lord. You have not betrayed my time in penury and allowed me to feel safe in Society again.'

He half turned to look at her with a slight smile. 'I'm as much on the edge of Society as you are.' Turning to face her, he explained, 'Although my friends have proved I was with them during the evening of the murder, so I could not have done it, I believe people still question my integrity. I fear my reputation has been besmirched forever.'

The colour intensified on Jemima's face, and she had to look away from his gaze. Was that not how she felt about him? Was he a dangerous man? How far could she trust him?

After a long pause, he sighed, and continued, 'You don't have to deny it, Jemima. I know it is the same for you.'

Unsure what to say, Jemima remained silent. What was the point of saying she did not think him a possible villain when she did? She knew so little about him. It would always be at the back of her mind that he might have committed the wicked deed he had been accused of. But she knew in her heart she did not see him as a rogue.

At last she looked up at his worried face and said, 'My lord, forgive my boldness when I say I have little knowledge of your character — although I am sure you know mine, after talking to Joe and tracking me down here.'

He nodded. 'Yes, I spoke to Joe's wife, who was full of praise for you and your work in Gin Lane. She told me about your bravery, adjusting to a poor woman's life and of the way you always helped those you could.'

'Sir, it is you we are supposed to be discussing.'

He chuckled and rubbed his chin. 'Indeed. You need to be reassured of my good character, that is the heart of the matter.'

'You need not tell me anything about yourself you do not wish to, and I am not one to gossip. However, one thing I have learned is that you are a private man, rarely seen in Society.'

Actually, Jemima had learned by listening to Society talk a little more about his circumstances — but only how rich he was and where he lived, and confirmation of his statements that he was not wed and was in want of a wife.

He gave a little cough and sat down again.

'I would be most surprised if you had not found out from your friends as much as you could about my circumstances — especially after I had proposed marriage to you!'

Jemima's self-control left her as her mouth fell open. She could hardly believe that he would mention that again. And she was afraid her coloured cheeks would tell him that was exactly what she had done. She hoped he did not think she been boasting to her friends that he had asked her to marry him — for she had not — nor mentioned how he had kissed her! These things were stored away in her private memories, too precious to her to be gossiped about.

He continued as though they were discussing a matter that could be resolved.

'When I received no reply from you about my offer — which I assure you was sincere and still is, but was badly thrown at you that evening — even though you did not refuse me, I appreciated you needed time to get to know me better before you made up your mind.'

Her heart leaped with joy, for he had not after all taken offence at her failure to say yes or no to his offer. Jemima could not deny that she longed to know more about him, but she sat looking at him, tongue-tied.

There was kindness in his smile, which eased her discomfort. 'I came here to make you another offer of a different kind . . . ' He suddenly stopped talking and put his hand to his ear. 'I think I can hear someone in the house.'

She frowned as she listened too.

Yes, indeed — there was a sound like a man's feet tramping along the hallway.

# 6

The sound of footsteps suddenly stopped and William went towards the door, grabbing hold of his cane, as if anticipating using it on the intruder.

A burglar came to Jemima's mind too, but soon her worry ceased as she heard her brother Charles call out, 'Jemima. Are you in?'

Her frown vanished as she called, 'I'm in the parlour, Charlie.'

Charles Perrot boomed, 'Where the hell are all your staff?' The door swung open and her tubby, red-faced brother entered the room staggering as he carried several large, flat boxes.

'I brought these boxes of fans just arrived from China for you to price before I set them out in the shop. I did not expect to have to cart them in here myself . . . why, good day, sir. I did not expect to find you with company,

114

either. I should go.'

William strode up, took the boxes from Charles and laid them on the table.

Charles, quickly assessing his sister's dapper visitor, said, 'Sir, I thank you for doing what a servant should be here to do.'

Jemima said with a giggle, 'Your lordship. This is my brother, Charles.'

Charles Perrot raised his eyebrows and bowed.

'I am honoured, my lord. You must be the Earl of Swanington my sister claims to know.' He took out his handkerchief to mop his brow.

'Indeed, I am.'

William assumed his lordly manner and for one awful moment Jemima felt he had taken a dislike to her brother; that Charles had suggested she had been gossiping about him when she had not.

'Your lordship,' said Charles, bowing his head deferentially, 'Forgive me for interrupting your conversation. I had no idea you were here — I saw no carriage outside.'

'Mr Perrot,' William said returning the bow. 'I am glad you have come, actually, for I was intending to speak with you.'

There was a silence as the men summed each other up like stags on the moors.

Good-naturedly, Charles smiled. 'Please say what you have to say, my lord, because I must get back to my shop.'

'It is a private matter.'

'Go ahead speak, m'lord.' Charles was used to dealing with the nobility in his shop and was not overawed. 'Ain't no one here. I understand my sister let all the servants run off this afternoon. Peculiar, but then my sister hired a rough bunch to run this house, and she's quite capable of dealing with anyone,'

Charles went up to Jemima and gave her a quick brotherly kiss on her cheek.

'I had better tell you straight then,' William said as he faced Charles, pulled back his shoulders, and said clearly, 'I wish to marry your sister.'

A gasp from Jemima made Charles look at her suspiciously.

'Not really surprised,' he said, 'I thought she'd been moping for some man ever since I got back from China and I presume you are that fellow.'

Crimson coloured Jemima's face, making her lift her hands to her cheeks to try to hide it.

William's smile showed his delight as he enquired, 'Then, sir, you have no objection to the marriage?'

Charles turned to Jemima asking, 'Do you really want to marry this nobleman, sister? He is not without rumours attached to him. I heard he was involved in some criminal activity.'

Jemima quickly retorted, 'He was cleared of any wrongdoing!'

'I am sure he was. otherwise he'd not be here for I know you are a good judge of character. The only objection I have is that anyone who has a blemish lurking around in their background might be ostracised by Society. And my wish is that, after your unfortunate times, you can now be secure. Content to be dancing, and shopping, and all the things ladies like to do, without a trail of gossip following you.'

Jemima valued her brother's kindly wish for her happiness, but wanted the same for William.

She said, 'I am in the same position as William, am I not? My reputation could be said to be as tarnished as his after my time in Gin Lane. Is that not so?'

Charles looked perplexed until William spoke up, 'One thing in our favour is that as a peer of the realm, I can do as I wish and my wife and I will be above Society. We need not heed the rules.'

Charles chuckled and said, 'Then as far as I am concerned you may certainly have my blessing to marry my dear, brave sister, if that is what you want — and if Jemima wants you too, of course.'

Jemima smiled a little self-consciously, knowing this was not a normal way of going about arranging a marriage — but then had anything been normal about what had happened to her in recent times?

Her gaze was captured by the man she felt in her heart was the man she wanted. His smile was inviting. But it was not his wealth or grand position she wanted. She loved him, although she did not fully understand why she had been instantly attracted to him, as it seemed he'd been attracted to her.

Yet she still could not bring herself to say, yes. She felt she still required more time to really get to know him, and to consider the change it would make in her life were she to accept his offer of marriage.

However, she did not have to explain her reluctance, nor even to reply, because William said, 'Now, I come to what I wish to discuss with you, sir. I have come to ask your sister to rescue me, to assist me to prove to her who it was who harmed my character, so she knows without doubt that I am innocent of the crime.'

'How can she do that, my lord?'

'By accepting an invitation to stay at the Dower House with my grand-mother, The Dowager Countess of Swanington, who hid me when there was a hue and cry to have me hanged. She will, no doubt, tell you everything about me from the first day I was able to walk, and will enjoy showing you my infant silver rattle!'

Jemima swallowed hard. She had successfully managed to survive in the slums of London for a while — but could she now do the opposite, and reside in the house of a grand old lady?

She knew she would have to if she wanted to be sure in her mind and to learn more about the man who wanted to marry her.

'Naturally,' William went on, 'You will wish to consider any possible dangers involved in helping me prove to you who was the murderer, as the person who has already killed once but, of course, I shall arrange for you to be well guarded and I shall be there, living in the main house nearby.'

Clearly this was to be no simple invitation for a visit to be looked over by his grandmother and other relatives. It would have an element of danger for a killer was loose in the vicinity, perhaps even in the very house where she would be staying!

Jemima clutched the arms of her chair. She felt as if she was about to leap off the church tower. Not only had she to consider marrying far above her station, but a man who was determined to find his maid's killer, so that she would feel unafraid to marry him.

The alternative was to stay in her safe home, bored and unfulfilled, without the man she felt sure she loved and wanted to marry.

Brother and sister looked at each other.

Jemima read the concern in her brother's eyes. He scratched his eyebrow, waiting for her opinion. When she seemed tongue-tied, he suggested, 'I have no objection to your going, Jemima, but you must decide if you wish to take on this challenge. You have already shown yourself to be brave and capable, but you have earned an easy gentlewoman's life now, and his lordship's invitation sounds as if it will be a little . . . adventurous. Think about it seriously. Now, I really must get back to work.'

Charles bowed his exit and clattered down the hall calling out to Jemima not to forget to price the fans.

'Well?' asked William when he had gone.

Jemima noted the anxiety in William's voice, the pleading in his eyes. He needed her to help him overcome his difficulties. He had a right to happiness just as she had. But it was her decision to take any risks involved in going to Swanington.

She took a long breath, then said, 'I should be delighted to meet your grandmother.'

William smiled. 'Thank you.'

She did not object to him coming near and putting his arms around her, drawing her close to his wide chest. For a full minute she was being held and could hear the beating of his heart. Her mind whirled with sensations of security and pleasure to be in his strong arms. He lowered his lips to touch hers for a few blissful moments.

Lost in the strengthening pressure of his arms around her, she clung to him.

'Oh William, I do love you,' she murmured, as his mouth moved to her ear and travelled down her throat in tiny, thrilling kisses.

Releasing her, he gave a deep sigh.

'I shall leave you now, Jemima, and arrange your visit with my grandmamma.' He bowed, smiled and winked at her as he picked up his hat and cane before he quickly left the room.

Agitated after the men had left the house, Jemima did not know what to do with herself and paced around the room.

So, the Earl of Swanington was serious about marrying her! He had formally asked her brother for her hand — and Charles had given his blessing. Charles was no fool and was used to assessing different types of people, even the nobility.

Hovering between feeling exultant to have been asked to marry the nobleman — again — still concerns about the offer deeply worried her.

Did she really love this man she had met by chance? Had he a clear conscience — or did he just want her to think it? Was she being fanciful to think he truly loved her? What could she offer him that he had not already, or was able to get?

Those questions might be answered if she went to Swanington Hall. She would not be staying with him in his grand house, but nearby with his grandmother, so her reputation would not be compromised.

She must brace herself and prepare to go.

Cluttering Jemima's mind were decisions she had to make quickly. The household must be arranged for in her absence, clothes had to be made — her dressmaker must be called. Jemima was almost panicking. In Gin Lane she wore any old garments but in noble surroundings, as guest of a grand lady she needed the correct wardrobe. She would consult her friend Sylvia, who had a lively interest in what fashionable women wore.

Awash with worries about the move she was about to make, Jemima suddenly pulled herself together. If she could manage life in Gin Lane then she should be able to manage living for a while in the dower house at Swanington Hall!

Many a young lady would be thrilled to receive such an invitation. She must be sensible and take one step at a time. The first one was to send a polite letter of acceptance in the correct etiquette she was taught at school, as the Countess of Swanington was sure to be a stickler.

Attempting to calm herself, she

opened the boxes of fans, carefully taking them out and spreading each one like giant butterflies to display their beautiful colours and designs.

*I shall ask Charles if he will allow me to take one of these beautiful fans to Sylvia as a present for her kindness to me. I wonder if Lady Swanington would appreciate a gift of a Chinese fan?*

Taking up a fan she fanned herself as she walked slowly around the room.

Such fantastic events had taken place in this room this day — from a boring existence as a spinster, to being the prospective wife of one of the greatest noblemen in the country.

But she couldn't ignore the burden William carried — a burden she had now agreed to share.

# 7

In the privacy of her boudoir, Sylvia was delighted to receive her gift of a fashionable Chinese fan — and even more excited to hear about Jemima's nobleman's proposal!

'Oh my, I can hardly believe it!' Sylvia kept repeating as if one of the wealthiest men in the land had proposed to her instead of her friend.

Jemima had not intended to tell Sylvia about the proposal, but she could no longer keep it to herself for it was like a pot boiling over inside her. 'You will keep it a secret, Sylvia?'

'Of course,' Sylvia replied promptly.

Jemima knew her friend was somewhat featherbrained, yet could be trusted. Sylvia had kept it secret from Society that the Perrots had to move to Gin Lane, and Jemima had no worry about her time there being exposed.

'I have been invited to stay with William's grandmamma, the Dowager Lady Swanington,' Jemima went on. 'And I am a trifle frightened.'

Sylvia raised her hands, clearly impressed.

'Oh my! I too would be more than a trifle frightened at the prospect of lodging with a lady so high in polite society.'

Jemima did not tell her the reason William wanted her to go there was to find a murderer, but said instead, 'I am invited there as a prospective bride — like a horse being bought at a horse dealers under inspection!'

Sylvia giggled. 'I cannot think of a young lady more capable of dealing with the ordeal than you, Jemima. I understand most girls have nerves about meeting their future in-laws.'

'I suppose so,' Jemima said. 'But I do seem to have extremes of life thrown at me of late.'

Both girls laughed.

Becoming more thoughtful, Jemima

said, 'You can help me, Sylvia.'

'How? You attended the same lessons in deportment and dancing as I.'

'I was thinking of my clothes . . . '

'Ah! You are talking about fashion which I love! Of course, your dress must be *très élégante.*'

Jemima frowned. 'I am not thinking of trying to look different from the way I dress now.'

'I should think not. If William likes you as you are, he will not want you to change your style. But we shall make sure you have the necessary gowns for all occasions. Now tell me, has Charles given you an extra allowance for your holiday wardrobe?'

'Charles is working hard to recover our father's losses. Although his new fan shop is thriving and he has been most generous to me, I should not like to be extravagant. I intend to choose garments I shall be able to wear after my ordeal.'

Why Jemima had chosen to use the word 'ordeal' to describe her coming visit to Swanington, she did not know. Probably because she knew there was much more to it than putting on fine clothes and minding her manners.

Sylvia was not to know that, and babbled on excitedly about the possibilities of what Jemima might wear and the best shops they should go to for buying the stuffs and the names of the dressmakers, shoe and hat makers she advised, saying finally, 'That should do you well enough until you marry the Earl of Swanington. Then your wardrobe can be expanded and you will be the envy of all women in Society!'

'I have yet to decide if I wish to marry him!'

'Oh, Jemima, you will! And I shall raise my own marriage prospects by knowing a countess!'

A bout of merriment sounded in the room, but soon the young ladies got down to the fun of planning an elegant yet serviceable wardrobe for Jemima to take away with her.

\* \* \*

William was overjoyed to return to Swanington and report to his grandmother that Miss Jemima Perrot would accept her invitation.

'I know you will like her,' he asured the elegant old lady when he visited her at the Dower House.

'That does not seem to be the point, my dear,' Lady Swanington replied as she moved gracefully about carrying a small watering can in her conservatory which housed the more delicate plants she took a delight in. She frequently took her meals in the sunny room.

William's mind was entirely on Jemima's visit as he sat in one of the squeaky basket chairs. His fingers idly fingered an orchid near him which reminded him of Jemima's soft skin.

'And what is the point, grandmama?'

Her ladyship watched an earwig scurrying along the window sill and replied, 'Whatever I think of the young lady, it is *you* who needs to like her.'

He sat up straight. 'Of course, I do — I love her, I have told you such.'

'And yet you bring her here . . . into danger.'

William frowned. 'She will have to come sometime if I marry her, which is what I want.'

His grandmother sighed and came to sit beside him. 'From what you have told me she seems a most unusual girl, recently overcome a year of hardship and does not need to land in another.'

'Are you saying that I should never marry? That the false accusation that I was a murderer will always prevent me from doing so?'

Looking into her grandson's worried eyes, she replied, 'There is nothing more I want now in this life than to see you happily married, William. But I do concern myself over the lady you choose.' She put up her delicate hand to prevent William from interrupting. 'Although Jemima seems to be the right choice for you, I wonder if it is the right choice for *her.*'

'She is free to make up her own mind — and as you know, she has not yet done so.'

'That is the point. She is sensible enough to realise that the maid's murderer is probably at large around here and so someone is still capable of harming you.'

William knew his grandmother spoke the truth. He remained silent.

Drawing in breath, her ladyship went on, 'You must not think I do not want Jemima to come here. I am looking forward to meeting your sweet girl. But I do wish to impress upon you that after years of looking after you, I am becoming older and less able and you must now take the reins and look after yourself and your chosen lady.'

William took his grandmother's hand and kissed it gently.

'I thank you for protecting me all my life, grandmamma. I love you dearly. And I am now ready to put on the coat of responsibility. I will leave you here among your flowers to enjoy your retirement. But I shall also make every effort to find the killer so that Jemima will know I am not guilty. In fact, she has told me she is willing for me to do that, and to help me, if she can.'

'And how are you planning to do such a thing?'

William grimaced. 'I know there are smugglers around my coastline — as there are all over the West Country — but I have reason to believe some are overstepping the mark. Perhaps the maid's killing was tied up with them. I will have to warn them to keep their heads down.'

'And how can you warn them, as you intend, when you do not know who they are?'

'A few on my estate must be part of a smuggling ring — they live too well to be relying solely upon the wages I give them.'

His grandmother looked at William's fresh young face and smiled. 'I never brought you up to be a fighter. You will be vulnerable.'

'I am the Earl, the landowner, they

will not dare to cross me. I have the power to have them all hanged and they know it. However, all I intend to do is confront and warn them. In return, if they know the killer, they are to tell me. That is fair.'

The dowager was not convinced. 'I just hope they do play fair. The majority of your estate men might be trustworthy — but one, or more, is not.'

William rose to his impressive height saying, 'That bad apple in the barrel will be rooted out. I have to prove I am capable of that or I will never be worthy of my position.'

'Take care, my dear. I did not bring you up to be slaughtered by a blackguard who likes brandy!'

William grinned and kissed his grandmama's cheek. 'Jemima is a fighter, even if I am not — you shall see,' he said airily.

The dowager, knowing he still had much to learn, prayed silently for him as she continued to tend her plants. He had to be responsible for his birthright.

She had not allowed him to be spoilt as a child, but he did have a terrible temper on occasion, and his behaviour when faced with villains had yet to be tested. She had given him time during his youth to enjoy his wealth and freedom, while she had dealt with the daily running of his estate. But the time had come for him to take the full burden from her hands.

* * *

Having left the Dower House, William rode back to his house — a hall built by his ancestor and too big for him alone. But it was his home and it could be altered to suit him as a family man with his wife and children to bring life and laughter into it.

First he had to take steps to secure the place.

Later, as he was dressing for dinner, he asked his valet Dykes if he knew where he might meet the local smugglers.

Dykes had been his valet since he was a schoolboy and he was excellent at his job of caring for the Earl's clothes and advising him on the art of dress, but his lack of charm made him difficult for the young nobleman to like and sometimes his straightforward manner meant William struggled to maintain the upper hand.

Dykes adjusted his lord's cravet saying, 'You want to know about our local smugglers? A rough lot so I've heard, m'lord.'

'You sound as if you might know some?'

'I dare say one or two fishermen who live by the coast might know something about them.'

'Make it known I wish to talk to them.'

'They won't tell you nothing!'

Being as tall as his valet, William swung round to glare eye-to-eye at his man.

'I think they will, when I make it clear I am after the maid's killer. They had better help me find out the truth or I shall send the lot of them to jail! Give that message to the servants — someone must know at least one of the smugglers.'

'I dare say you're right about that, m'lord.'

As Dykes began to brush the earl's coat, William added, 'I intend to marry, Dykes, and my betrothed is to visit my grandmother at the Dower House. Miss Perrot is a young lady of great resourcefulness — she will help me to sniff out the killer. Make that known downstairs, too.'

'I will, m'lord.'

After Dykes had opened the door for his lordship to go downstairs, he began to tidy the room and put out a nightshirt. He muttered to himself, 'He has no idea what's been going on behind his back — nor his grandmother.'

Dykes knew the smugglers were so well organised that if William dared interfere he would be the next to die

— and that betrothed of his too, if she were nosy.

Smuggling was a sport in the West Country, and during the earl's childhood it had been easy to persuade local fishermen to take part or at least keep their mouths shut. But now the earl was fully grown, he would be a danger to the smuggling ring. Dykes would have to skip off with the assets. But a consignment was due, and he resolved to wait for that lucrative haul before he left.

They would never find out who had murdered that nosy maid. Only he knew — because he had done it.

★   ★   ★

William felt buoyant. He was young, fit and in love. He felt he was well able to take charge of his inheritance now that he had reached the age of maturity. Now that he had let it be known that he was going to investigate the murder he had been accused of, he was keen to get started.

Dykes was sure to spread the word that he was going to spend his time investigating the smuggling taking place on his coastline. The operation had become too big and he suspected it involved more that a few bottles of brandy being bought ashore occasionally. It had to be curbed.

William also suspected the poor little maid had discovered more than was good for her to know and so had been silenced.

If the blame had not been put on him, the unsolved murder mystery might have been forgotten in time. But whoever had done it had tried to shift the blame onto him, thinking he was unable to do anything about it.

There they were wrong.

William knew he had still much to learn about mastering his character — he was like like a raw recruit ready to be turned into an officer — yet he was a young man of resolve and a great determination to get to the truth of the matter.

And he wanted to marry, but first he wanted to clear up this stain on his character that had been put on him.

He suddenly felt the urgency of his quest, for his body ached to be joined with his love, Jemima — and she needed to be assured that he would be worthy of her love, without a blemish on his reputation.

# 8

There was much packing to do when Jemima's clothes were ready and the date of travelling decided on.

A lady had to be accompanied by her maid, and although Peggy was far from being a trained ladies' maid, Jemima told her she would be pleased to have her.

However she warned her, 'Peggy, I hope Lady Swanington's servants are not unkind to you. They may look down on you, being untrained as you are. But it is a grand opportunity for you to learn how to behave by watching Lady Swanington's maids. A ladies' maid is a very good position to have in a grand household.'

Fortunately, Peggy was in agreement. Her inferior background and lack of knowledge about how high-born ladies behaved did not seem to bother her.

Nor did the snubs she was warned she might get from the Dowager's superior servants. 'I reckon I'm as good as any of 'em,' she told Jemima.

'Yes, indeed you are, Peggy. But you will be like me, unused to living in a grand house filled with servants. The men will wear livery, and the maids have black dresses with pretty aprons, so like me, you will require some new clothes.'

Jemima was pleased to see Peggy was enthusiastic about the venture ahead of them but warned her, 'We must tread carefully and try not to upset anyone.'

'Yes, miss.'

'You must say ma'am, not miss.'

'Yes, miss. I mean ma'am.'

Jemima smiled. Peggy was at least willing if not competent. 'I must warn you of something else.'

Peggy stopped folding her mistress's clothes into the travelling trunk. 'What's that, ma'am?'

Jemima knew she couldn't avoid telling Peggy of her fears that the murderer was at large and could strike again.

'We'll be staying at the Dower House, where the Dowager Countess of Swanington lives. I think you should know that a maid was murdered recently at the big house at Swaninton, where the Earl of Swaninton lives.'

Jemima wasn't surprised the news of a murder didn't seem to affect Peggy as the girl had been brought up in a district where murders were not uncommon. She looked enquiringly at her maid to see if the girl showed any qualms, having been told about the worrying situation.

Peggy noticed Jemima was looking at her intently and stared back. Then as she put the last of the clothes in the trunk and closed the lid, she said, 'I'll look after you, miss. You needn't be finking about fings like that. It ain't anyfing to do wif us — we're going on 'oliday, ain't we?'

Grateful for her maid's common sense, and adopting the same attitude to any other possible dangers she may face, Jemima smiled. Peggy's willingness to learn, as well as her good nature, made her a perfect companion.

The next day as they departed from London on the public transport. Jemima reminded Peggy, 'We needn't pretend to be any different from what we are.'

'Yes, ma'am, we're just two London birds flown off to the West Coast to be by the seaside for a while,' agreed Peggy, helping her mistress up the steps into the coach.

Jemima chuckled, but it didn't mean she wasn't worried about what lay ahead of her. She had told Peggy nothing of the tremendous step in her life Jemima was contemplating, of her passion for the Earl of Swanington, though she suspected Peggy knew.

Jemima had prepared herself as well as she could. Her travelling trunk was heaved up onto the roof of the coach with the other travellers' luggage. As she sat in the coach with Peggy and their carpet bags, being bounced along the country lanes after leaving the streets of London, she hoped she had not forgotten anything of importance.

It was a shame, Jemima thought, that she did not own any jewellery which would have enhanced hergowns, but all her mama's precious pieces had been lost in the fire. Although she had borrowed a necklace from Sylvia, jewellery was, in Jemima's opinion, more than decoration. It needed to be given and treasured as a gift from someone you love. She always thought it sad when she had to price pawned gold rings and other personal items, knowing the pain of those having to part with them, even for a short period.

As the carriage got underway Jemima felt excited about getting away from London and the joy of viewing the beautiful English countryside in summertime — but most of all, seeing William again. It proved to her that she needed him as much as he said he needed her. Her maid might think of it as a holiday but she knew her trip had a serious purpose.

'Oh, Miss, look at that!' Peggy was

full of amazement at seeing the country for the first time in her life. 'Look there, those men are building a little 'ouse with yellow straw!' she cried out as she pointed to a haystack. Her remarks amused the other travellers in the coach.

Jemima was learning too. She had not travelled far out of London before, and the peaceful fields, woodlands, rivers and hamlets she saw in the sunshine entranced her. What she saw calmed her and prepared her for what she anticipated would be some sort of test.

Her life was at the crossroads — which way would it go?

★   ★   ★

'Swanington seems a long way orf,' remarked Peggy after several days of travelling, two overnight stays at post houses, and many breaks to change the horses.

It certainly seemed as if they were going to the back of beyond, as they were the only passengers to have continued on the journey at the last post house. Jemima just hoped that a carriage would be there to meet them at their destination.

'Cor, look at all that water, Miss!' exclaimed Peggy as the coach horses trotted along the coastal path towards the village of Swanington.

It was a thrill for the two young women to see the sun shining on the blue sea. Although familiar with the brown River Thames, neither of them had seen the sea before.

Their enjoyment at seeing the vast open water revived Jemima after the long journey. She felt ready to face the next stage in her life. Whether she was going to be the mistress of this estate near the sea, she did not yet know, but she, couldn't prevent herself from longing to see the owner again.

Arriving at the post house at the village of Swanington, the end of the long journey, they dismounted from the coach, feeling the sharp costal wind that seemed to penetrate their travel cloaks and make them shiver.

The thrill of seeing the seaside disappeared as Jemima looked at the dark, racing clouds and wondered if a storm was brewing. How far was it to the Dower House, and how were they going to get there?

★   ★   ★

Seated in the post house, where they were out of the wind and enjoying a jug of coffee and fruit buns, Jemima was about to ask the landlord about obtaining transport when she heard her name being called.

'Miss Perrot! Miss Perrot!'

'She's over 'ere!' yelled Peggy before Jemima could restrain her.

Startled to see a smartly dressed young gentleman approaching them, followed by a lady of quality, Jemima swallowed nervously, but her apprehension turned to relief when she saw their gracious smiles.

'Welcome to Swanington, Miss Perrot,' the buck said as he and his lady bowed, and obliged Jemima to get to her feet and do the same.

'Miss Perrot, my sister and I are pleased to meet you at last. William asks to be forgiven as he is unable to be here to greet you. He asked me to escort you to the Dower House and told me to tell you he looks forward to seeing you soon.'

Mixed thoughts tumbled through Jemima's head as he went on to introduce himself and his sister as Mary and Tom Corbishire, neighbours and great friends of the earl.

At once Jemima felt she liked them both and was pleased to accept their invitation to be taken in their carriage to the Dower House, even though she was disappointed to learn William had better things to do.

'I expect William has many commitments,' she remarked when they were seated in Tom's coach and on their way.

'Please do not think he did not want

to come and collect you, Miss Perrot. William was most upset he could not come,' exclaimed Tom. 'I know he has great affection for you.'

'He does indeed,' assured Mary nodding and smiling at Jemima. 'He is determined to remove any doubts he fears you may have about him.'

Amazed to hear that William had confided his feelings about her to his friends, Jemima was unable to say anything for a while, but her curiosity aroused, she eventually asked, 'I expect he has told you a great deal about me.'

'No, Miss Perrot, he has not said much other than you are a courageous and kind young lady.'

'Yes, she is!' declared Peggy.

The maid's interruption reminded them to refrain from discussing personal matters in front of servants.

'We have been looking forward to getting to know you,' Mary said diplomatically.

*And I feel I will enjoy your companionship*, thought Jemima, content to think she had already found out that William had good friends, and whatever he had told them about her circumstances, they wished to be her friends too.

'Look, you can see Swanington Hall through the trees.' Tom instructed Jemima to look out of the carriage window as the horses clip-clopped by the home of the Earl of Swanington.

It was as Jemima had imagined the hall would be, an impressive sight. Looking over a shimmering lake in the foreground at the enormous classical style house with an astonishing number of windows, Jemima thought it would be a full time job for a man to clean them all.

William had inherited that vast building. Such impressive grandeur was more of a responsibility to have, than a possession she would ever want.

The Dower House in the grounds nearby was much smaller but similar, built by the same workman under the directions of the architect who had designed the big house. It echoed many features of the famous Chateau of Versailles in France.

The Dower House was like the smaller houses of the Trianons — just as beautiful — but the smaller house seemed preferable to live in.

Arriving there, it seemed like a sanctuary, not only for her and her maid to end their travelling, it also enabled her to get away from the rain which had started. Jemima was not surprised for she had been told Devon's green countryside was due to its copious rainfall, especially in late springtime.

Struck by the warmth coming from a house that was loved and lived in, Jemima understood why it was the place where William had gone for shelter when the law had been snapping at his heels.

# 9

The Dowger Countess of Swanington, when Jemima met her, turned out to be far less intimidating than she had expected her to be, although every inch a lady in her deportment and elegant style of dress. Once a beauty, she still retained her fine looks with a kindly twinkle in her eyes, and greeted Jemima warmly.

Jemima was able to forget her worry about being treated as a merchant's daughter, and even having to watch her manners, as the grand lady seemed genuinely pleased to see her. Soon Jemima found it easy to relax and talk to her as they sat in her drawing room and sipped tea.

'How unfortunate it was for your papa to have his shop burned down,' the lady said, 'but I have learned that your brother has recouped his business well.'

Jemima was not surprised that

William had told his grandmother about her unfortunate circumstances after the fire, but, not wanting to dwell on her troubles of the past, she said, 'Yes, indeed, ma'am. I am proud of the way Charles has built up the shop again . . . which reminds me, I have brought you a fan, recently arrived from China, which I hope you might like.'

Removing the fan box from her travel bag, Jemima gave the countess her gift.

Opening the box, the lady exclaimed, 'Why, how thoughtful you are to bring me a such a lovely gift!' She picked the fan out of the box, and spread it out to admire the ivory pierced sticks and medallions of coloured Chinese scenes and motifs. Picking it up, she fanned herself with practised ease showing she had used one before.

'The Chinese are so skilled at making such things,' explained Jemima, delighted to find her present gave the countess pleasure. 'Their designs are popular with ladies of fashion in London. You may know that the Chinese artistic style is called Chinoiserie, and the Prince of Wales has built a Pavilion in Brighton filled with Chinese art.'

The countess was keen to hear from Jemima all she knew, and then they went on to discuss the variety of fans that were available. Having a subject that interested them both was useful in allowing them to get to know each other. But as the time for the evening meal approached, and time for the ladies to change for dinner, the countess suddenly looked concerned.

'It is getting very late. Cook will be worried about the food being over-cooked. I wonder where William is? He is supposed to be coming here for dinner tonight.'

Jemima began to wonder too.

'Ring the bell-pull please, Jemima, and I shall ask the butler if he has arrived. I cannot think what has delayed him. It is not like him to be discourteous by being late when we have guests.' She looked at Jemima and added, 'Especially as his much-loved lady is waiting for him.'

A hot flush spread over Jemima's face. She was both pleased to know, yet embarrassed to think, that William had confided his love for her to his grandmother.

As they waited, she felt free to ask questions about William, and learned his parents had died in a carriage accident, leaving William as a small boy with the enormous house, land and wealth.

'And with some relatives — including an heir we do not like — who have shown him nothing but unkindness when he was growing up.'

How dreadful that an orphaned boy should have been treated badly by some of his own relatives!

That, Jemima thought, would account for the young earl seeming to be cautious in his dealings with people. It might also explain why William was not yet married.

His grandmother leaned forward and almost whispered, 'Can you believe that some of our relatives were keen to spread false rumours about William's good name?

I think they are jealous, keen to get hold of his wealth. Not one of them came to his aid when he was accused of murder. I fear they wanted rid of him so that they could inherit his title and estate.'

Jemima could believe it, and any amount of man's evil, after her unusual education in Gin Lane. She nodded. 'That was a terrible thing to do! He was in danger of being hanged!'

'Yes, indeed. So, I have had to protect him myself as far as I am able to.'

Jemima, reflecting for a moment or two, said, 'I expect it was his fortune that made him a victim.'

'I think you understand very well the difficulties William has had growing up. People think that, being wealthy, William has a charmed life with every-thing he wants, but that is not so. He has responsibilities. Many people rely on him for a living, but now he is a young man I have been keen to let him have some freedom, so I have been over-seeing much of the estate to let him enjoy his youth. He loves sailing.'

Jemima nodded and smiled as she pressed her lips together. It seemed to her her hostess was not trying to hide anything from her, that the grand lady felt they were on a different footing from that of the earl's female friend coming to stay and be judged by his grandmother. No, a serious matter was spoiling his future — and his need to marry and beget an heir.

The Countess continued, 'William is a man of honour and is gradually learning to make a success of his estate and has good friends, but I think he needs a sensible wife to stand by him.'

Jemima's cheeks reddened as the ladies exchanged sympathetic smiles.

'Now we shall dress for dinner,' her hostess said, looking at the ornate clock on the mantelpiece anxiously — because William still had not appeared. Rising, she rang the bell-pull and smiled at Jemima. 'I shall ask my housekeeper to show you to your bedchamber and find your maid. I do hope you will be comfortable staying here with us, my dear.'

It was a kind gesture and Jemima appreciated why William thought so highly of his grandmother.

★ ★ ★

When the hour struck eight and William still had not arrived the ladies, dressed in their evening finery, were waiting to go in for their evening meal and looked at each other with worried expressions. The dowager countess frowned as she pressed her lips together in consternation.

'What could be keeping him?'

They had been chatting together to pass the time. After the ladies waited another quarter of an hour, she called the butler and enquired again if the earl had arrived or had left a message. On being told the servants knew nothing, the ladies went into the dining room, and ate their evening meal together without male company. Although Jemima was hungry after her long journey, and the food was delicious — and Lady

160

Swanington a charming hostess — missing William spoiled the evening.

Jemima tried to hide her disappointment by talking in a cheerful, lively way. Her ladyship had friends in the neighbourhood but as she had retired from high social life some time ago, she enjoyed hearing about the latest London chit-chat and fashions, adding her own reminisces about amusing incidents during her time in Society.

After dinner, Lady Swanington apologised to Jemima, saying, 'I am sure William has good reason to be absent, my dear. By morning he should be here after breakfast and be keen to show you around his house and estate.'

As her ladyship retired early, Jemima did too — having no company.

The guest bedroom had striped wallpaper and was elegantly furnished with white wood and Jemima found it comfortable with a large feather bed. But a restful night was not forthcoming, as Peggy burst into the bedroom to inform her that a message had arrived for her from William.

'Where is the message, Peggy?'

'There ain't nothing to give you, just to tell you, miss,' Peggy replied,

Putting down her hairbrush, as she had taken down her dressed hair for evening, and was brushing it ready for night time, Jemima asked, 'What did he say?'

Peggy shook her head. 'He weren't there.'

Becoming annoyed, Jemima felt like shaking her maid, but controlled her temper to ask, 'What is all this about? You said there was a message from the earl for me. Now what is it?'

Peggy looked a little scared hearing the unusually sharp tone of her mistress's voice.

She replied, 'It was a lad what came to the kitchen door, Miss, while me and the other servants was finishing our evening meal. He said, his lordship had told him to say, 'Come to the Mill at midnight'.'

Frustrated by the ridiculous request, Jemima could have screamed, but she remembered that Peggy was in a strange household.

'Peggy, we are both tired after our long journey today, and being in a new house with people we don't know. Now are you sure someone was not jesting with you? Or the boy got the message wrong, or was telling a lie?'

Peggy looked confused. 'No, I don't think so, Miss. I saw him myself and I think the boy was serious about what he was saying, I'm sure he was. He repeated that he was told to give the message to you and only you. But when I said Miss Perrot had retired, he looked really narked about it. Said he would get a whipping and wouldn't get his money if she didn't get the message. So I said I was your maid and would tell you.'

Puzzled, Jemima asked, 'What did the other servants say about it?'

'Only the butler came to the door

with me and heard what the lad and me was talking about. We discussed it when the boy had gone. He's ever such a nice man, is Mr Sprott. He told me that when the young earl was hiding from the law, when the lawmen came around, his lordship hid in Swanington Mill. So he said it sounded as if he might be in trouble again.

'Even so, he said he would strongly advise you not to go but that I was to tell you about the message, anyway.'

Greatly alarmed by this stark request and the possibility that William was in trouble, Jemima paced up and down the bedroom, agitated to decide what she should do.

A gentleman would never ask a lady to go out and meet him alone at night! William, who said he loved her, would not have sent such a message. But could it be true that he needed her?

'We'd better go, Miss,' she heard Peggy say. 'You never know what them aristocrats get up to — and he might need 'elp.'

Jolted out of her reverie, Jemima knew her maid was right — she would not sleep a wink if she tried to ignore the message.

She loved William — she had come to Swanington for that reason. He told her he wanted to marry her but that he could not expect her to accept when he still had trouble surrounding him.

Although an earl with enormous power in the vicinity, he was vulnerable. Whoever had murdered his maid was still free and capable of harming him. Now that he had asked for her to meet him at midnight at Swanington Mill, she could not refuse to go there.

Potential dangers bombarded her mind. Of course, it was possible that she would be walking into trouble but she did not think William would play silly games with her or want to endanger her. Besides, he knew she was used to being careful and avoiding danger when she lived in the London Dockland.

Jemima made up her mind. She had

come to Swanington to find out all she could about William, after all.

'I agree I ought to go, Peggy, but I shall need something to wear. I have nothing suitable — '

'Righto, miss! I'll find you some maid's clothes. And a cloak wif a hood, cos it's still raining.'

Peggy was gone before Jemima had time to say anything else. As she waited for her maid to return, Jemima went to the window and looked out at the night sky.

Was she being foolish to even think of venturing out on this stormy night? Was she being tricked into leaving the house? And yet how would she know if the call for help was genuine unless she went out to see if the man she loved needed her assistance?

She was anxious to see William. He had not turned up for the evening meal — why was that?

At least wearing clothes like a maid would give her some means to hide her identity and to slip about unnoticed.

In less than quarter of an hour Peggy was back and Jemima dressed quickly so that the two women were cloaked and looked like two servants. Jemima felt nervous stepping furtively out of her bedroom in the darkness, knowing it was not the proper behaviour expected of a guest, especially dressed in disguise as a servant girl.

# 10

Jemima flitted downstairs with Peggy carrying a flickering candle, as the grandfather clock in the dark house sounded. Thirty minutes past eleven.

Creeping through the darkened hall downstairs, the last person Jemima expected to meet was Lady Swanington, looking not unlike a ghost dressed in her white night clothes.

'Your ladyship . . . I, em . . . ' faltered Jemima feeling terribly embarrassed as she gave the lady a curtsy. Her nervousness made her hand wobble and she almost dropped her candlestick — only the butler who was with the dowager countess swept forward and took it from her hand.

Jemima knew that dressing in maid's clothes and wandering about the house in the midnight hours, was enough for her to be told to leave. It was certainly not the conduct expected of guests in a country house.

She was relieved when she heard the countess say, 'Jemima, my dear, my butler gave me the message William sent you. Sprott was most anxious about you venturing out, as of course, am I.'

Jemima regained some of her wits after being shocked to meet the older lady and replied, 'Ma'am, I am so sorry to have disturbed your sleep. I was unsure what to do when I was given the message. It was by word of mouth, and I was wondering whether it was indeed William who had sent for me or . . . you see, I am not unaware that he is hunting for the person who killed one of his maids, and he may require assistance.

'As he did not arrive for dinner, he may have found himself in difficulties. As you know, my maid and I are not unused to moving about in the worst crime-ridden areas of London where I used to live. So I felt I must take the risk and find out if his lordship needs heip.'

'Very commendable, my dear. I am sure you know at times I hid him in the Mill when he was being hunted by the law.'

Jemima removed a strand of her hair that had fallen untidily over her nose and tucked it behind her ear. She knew she looked as undressed as her hostess, yet she felt less concerned now that her appearance was being judged, as the reason for her subterfuge was being discussed.

'Yes, ma'am, he did say you hid him at times.'

'Just as you helped him, I understand, when he was trying to board a ship in the London docks, and he fell off the coach then had the mishap of being robbed.'

Jemima relaxed at little, knowing her ladyship knew all about the incident and probably had learned from William about her being dressed like a maid in the Dockland.

'Now,' Lady Swanington said coming closer so that Jemima could see the worry etched on her face, 'I think you may be right, Jemima. I have the feeling that William may be in danger again. I do not know what it is all about, but the message by word of mouth is possibly incorrect.'

'Yes, I thought it might be too,' Jemima said, 'But I felt I had to go to the Mill — oh, but I don't even know where it is . . . ' She realised how stupid she must sound and added, 'I suppose it was silly of me . . . '

'No, my dear.' The old lady, to her surprise, came forward and kissed Jemima on the cheek, 'You are a very brave young gel, willing to come to my grandson's aid when he calls for help. Although it was a strange way to send you a message at this time of night as it makes your conduct seem most improper and I am sure he would not have done that unless he was desperate — or the message did not come from him. You are a true friend of William, my dear, but you need protection too.'

Reminded of their intended mission, Jemima gave a shiver and said, 'It must be approaching midnight. I should go, ma'am.'

'You will not go alone,' the countess said. 'I have assembled some men to accompany you.' She signalled for the side door to be opened, and Jemima could see a group of estate men, carrying lanterns, waiting outside the house.

Somewhat comforted at the thought of being escorted to the Mill, and knowing her hostess was approving of her going, Jemima explained, 'I dressed as a maid so that I would be less noticeable.'

'A very wise thing to do. Nevertheless, I will be praying for your safe return by morning. For I do not know why William wants you at the Mill, nor what awaits you when you get there. Now I shall leave you in the capable hands of the earl's estate men who have assembled to find him because they like and respect him. And they are willing to assist and protect his chosen lady too.'

Embarrassed and bewildered to think all those men knew that William was considering marrying her, Jemima could think of nothing to say. She curtsied to Lady Swanington who whispered, 'God bless you, my dear,' before she turned and vanished into the dark recesses of the corridor.

Trying to hide her apprehension, Jemima took a deep breath as she braved the rain and stepped out into the starry night. Linking arms with Peggy as maids often did, they joined the men who set off down the long tree-lined drive. The strong wind made their cloaks dance about in the chilly air as steady light rain misted the countryside. Peggy seemed overawed by the night time walk in strange territory. Usually chatty, she held her mistress's arm in silence.

'How far is Swanington Mill?' Jemima asked the man who had come to walk beside her. He was the man in charge, as he had given the order for some men to walk ahead leading the way. He carried a lantern as some other men did, showing the way as the party moved swiftly.

'It isn't far, ma'am. Only a couple of miles.'

Peggy chuckled as she was used to walking, as Jemima gave a pained sigh. Since returning to an easy life of a lady, she had become soft and unused to the hard exercise working women had.

But Jemima found the walk invigorating. The damp night air dispelled the tiredness she had felt earlier. Her maid's boots enabled her to trudge easily along paths and get over stiles to cross meadows with the group of men.

Coming near to a silvery river, they all stopped. The rain had eased so that the women could throw off their hoods to look around.

'There's the Mill, ma'am.'

Looking to where the man pointed, Jemima could just make out the silhouette of a tall building by the river ahead.

'Now what do we do, miss?' Peggy asked.

Jolted by the question, Jemima clenched her fists with a sudden fright. Aware everyone was looking at her. Her immediate reaction was to say, *I know not*, but she knew that was not the answer she was expected to give. The earl had sent the message for *her* to come, not everyone else. She had to decide, now that the mill was in sight, what she should do.

Jemima knew, as his lordship's chosen lady, she was expected to show leadership. She would have to give orders to the servants, run the domestic side of the earl's estate. This was a testing time for her. She would have to be brave, walk by herself to search for William in the Mill.

Taking a deep breath and wishing her voice did not sound as if she was as afraid as she felt, she said, 'I . . . I think I should go ahead by myself and see if I can find his lordship.'

No one disagreed.

'I'll come with you, Miss,' piped up Peggy.

With her tough little maid willing to accompany her, Jemima felt strengthened. And knowing the small army of men would be nearby, the two women set out to follow the river bank to the mill.

Jemima and Peggy, as citizens of London, found all the sights and sounds of nature were strange to them. Their knowledge of the seedy side of London was so different yet it made them cautious as they approached the looming mill.

Aware the nocturnal wildlife — badgers and water vole — were afoot, with the occasional cry of some animal and rustle of the bulrushes as they passed, Jemima was acutely aware that they were treading towards an unknown situation.

'Stay where you are!'

A commanding voice in the darkness made both women almost jump out of their skins.

Jemima was relieved to see William's tall figure emerge from a clump of alders ahead of them. In the half-darkness he seemed to be wearing his finest evening dress, which Jemima thought strange, as he had not arrived at dinner.

'Cor! You didn't half give me a fright!' shrilled Peggy without thinking.

'Hush, girl!'

Jemima was delighted to see William but walking nearer, she could see his lordship was not alone. Three men were lurking behind him.

Without properly greeting her, William suddenly turned away and marched on ahead towards the mill. The women were immediately surrounded by the men and were obliged to follow behind.

The mill door stood open for them to enter.

Hesitating, because Jemima suddenly sensed something was not right, she stood still — until a hard push in her back pitched her forward into the mill.

# 11

Once inside the mill, Jemima's eyes searched for William's figure among the men in the dark, dusty interior which was lit only by one lantern hitched to a post.

'Oh!' she shrieked, gripped by fear as she realised she had been tricked.

The man she thought was William — a tall man stylishly dressed in the Earl of Swanington's evening clothes — was not William at all. He was an impostor! He had fooled them into believing he was the earl.

'Lordy!' Peggy cried, 'You ain't 'is lordship!'

She immediately received a slap in the face from the impostor.

Peggy opened her mouth and let out a fearful screech and was silenced by another blow.

Jolted to see such a cruel act of

unnecessary violence against her maid, Jemima stood protectively in front of the sobbing Peggy, fearful in case the girl began to attack the man who had insulted and hurt her. She knew Peggy was capable of flying like a wild cat at him — she had seen women fight in Gin Lane!

Her suspicions about who had sent her the message to come to the mill were unravelling, and in the back of her mind Jemima feared this bully could well be the man who had killed the Swanington maid. With her mouth quivering in fright, she said as boldly as she could, 'Who are you? Where is his lordship?'

The men around began to guffaw, which made Jemima's heart sink. What had they done with William?

'He's tied up nice and tight. And there he'll stay. And you two nosy maids can join him until I decide what to do with you. I'd like to know where that woman of his is — the one from London. Far too grand to come here, is she? Hiding with his grandmother and sent you two maids instead?'

At once Jemima realised the men did not know who she was, she hoped Peggy would not let it slip. Let them think she was a servant girl.

His sneering voice sounded ominous. 'We'll lock 'em up with his lordship, and set fire to the mill after we've moved our business.'

'No, don't kill 'em, Dykes!' a man's voice yelled out. 'There's been enough hue and cry about the maid you dispatched.'

'Shut up, you fool, or you'll join them!'

The other men grumbled but none spoke up.

Wild thoughts raced through Jemima's mind. She noted Dykes was the leader and ruled by fear. He was dressed in the earl's clothes, pretending to be him. And the earl had been captured — imprisoned — and they were all in real danger of being burned alive!

Suddenly Jemima felt her arms being pulled behind her, making her cry out in protest when she felt her wrists bound tightly together. Truly captured, she struggled helplessly.

She could hear Peggy squawking like an affronted chicken, 'Let me go! Lemme go, you great louts!' Then her voice faded and Jemima feared they had silenced her, remembering what had happened to another maid at Swanington, and dreading to think how these rough men had harmed Peggy. The brutes! And she had led Peggy into this trap!

Terrified to think what they may do to her if she dared object, Jemima cringed remained silent, helpless — at their mercy. And what state was her love William in?

Jemima was soon to know as she was dragged towards another door. A brawny man opened it, and she was roughly pushed inside. In the dim light from the lantern the men carried, she saw a body lying on the floor of the storeroom full of sacks of flour. Anguish overwhelmed her when she recognised William, the Earl of Swanington, lying on the floor in a sorry state. His evening clothes had been removed — obviously taken and worn by the man Jemima had first thought was him, but now knew as Dykes.

'Oh no!' she gasped, sickened to see signs of the fight he had been in, as William's underclothes were ripped and bloodstained. When she was near enough, she could see his face showed signs of having been cruelly hit and battered — and he appeared unconscious. Her heart bled for him and tears formed in her eyes.

After the men left, taking the lantern, Jemima moved awkwardly in the darkness with her hands tied, to kneel by him.

'William,' she whispered bending over and kissing his cold cheek, 'I came to find you.'

He recognised her voice and mumbled, 'Oh, Jemima! What an idiot I have been to put you in such danger!'

He appeared to have a black eye and a bleeding mouth, and was clearly suffering. As tears filled her eyes, she explained, 'You did not put me in danger — I know you would not do that! I chose to come here when I received your message.'

William asked, puzzled, 'What message?'

Jemima now knew now for sure that she had been tricked but was not entirely surprised as she had suspected the message may not have been sent by him. 'When you did not arrive for dinner, it was my decision to look for you.'

He groaned. He seemed unable to say anything more coherently. His injuries seemed more severe than the first time she had rescued him after he had fallen off the coach in Gin Lane. It was as if he had used the last of his strength.

Kissing his forehead and bleeding lips gently, she whispered, 'Do not try to talk now. Your estate men are outside and will be coming to rescue us soon.'

He rallied a little, lifting his head and shoulders as he tried to speak but fell back murmuring, 'Warn them . . .'

How could she? Even if the estate men knew the earl was here, needing to be rescued, how could they come to their aid with the gang of ruffians in the mill?

If only her hands were not tied!

'William, I cannot move much — I am tied up, as you are.'

Perhaps they would die together?

Jemima did not tell him about her worry about Peggy. What would be the use? He was exhausted with pain and remorse. She lay down close to him. Like lovers prevented from showing their love, and yet face to face they could nuzzle up to each other.

It was this intimate togetherness that gave Jemima a strange contentedness. Nothing else mattered during those hours they lay on the hard floor of the store room, overcoming their pain by murmuring their love for each other.

If they were to die, at least they were together, and her love for him was shown as best she could. He had been tortured, battered, and perhaps seriously hurt by those smugglers — because she felt sure that was what they were up to — but he would know he was loved.

★   ★   ★

'Jemima!' William's urgent voice awoke her.

Stiff and uncomfortable, she could see his anxious face looking at her as there was light coming through the storeroom window. It must be the morning sunrise.

'William . . . are you better?'

He smiled ruefully and said, 'I feel dreadful. Beaten up and sore all over.'

'Who are those cruel men?'

'All local men by the sound of their accents. Some from my estate, I expect.' He let out a cry of anguish. 'I've always tried to be fair to my men! Why have they treated me like this?'

'There must be a reason for their betrayal.'

'Yes, indeed. They are smugglers, I've discovered, afraid I might report them to the constables. But landowners along the coast know some smuggling takes place and ignore it. I do too, so what has made them turn against me?'

He sounded so hurt that some of his men had harmed him, that Jemima felt sorry for him. She said, 'One man seems to be in charge. A man called Dykes. Do you know him?'

William gasped in betrayed surprise.

'Yes, indeed I do — he is my valet.'

'He sounds a real villain — the others seem afraid of him.'

William groaned, 'You are quite right, Jemima. Until tonight I had no idea what power he was wielding. I have been lying here thinking for hours. And I have reasoned out that the leader — Dykes, I now know — has had the opportunity to organise a giant smuggling ring while I have been pursuing my interest in sailing. I am frequently away from home, and he has had the time to impose his will on others.' William gave a cry of discomfort, then continued, 'Such a man is power-mad. Insane. I understand now. Dykes is cruel and greedy. He wants to grasp all he can and he manipulates others — he killed a maid who had discovered what he has been doing. And clearly it was he who blamed me for her death, and told others to do the same.'

'He has access to your clothes and impersonates you.'

'Oh Jemima, I have been so blind!'

Even if they were to be slaughtered, Jemima wanted William to know that she did not blame him for Dykes's wrongdoing.

'No, no, my darling. You were young and inexperienced. When your maid was killed and you were accused of murder, you tried to find out who had done it. Dykes took advantage of you. He must be stopped. We must free ourselves as he has the intention of emptying the mill of his contraband and then setting fire to this place.'

William's eyes closed in agony.

Jemima looked at the crushed nobleman, knowing he was a good man. He had simply been unfortunate with the man who had been chosen to be his valet, who had taken advantage of him.

She had to save him. She was not going to allow that dreadful fate to befall him, or Peggy, or herself!

But what could she do to prevent it? Jemima had to think of something to free them — and quickly. She could see that he was roped up tightly, but . . .

'If I get my hands near yours, can you untie my hands? They have used thinner rope on me.'

Jemima moved to show him her bound arms and hands that now ached and had begun to bleed where she had chafed them as she tried to release the cutting rope.

Neither of them could control their gasps of pain as William moved himself and struggled to release Jemima's firmly bound arms and hands. Still very weak, he explained the situation they were in as he worked away with his fingers and teeth to gnaw at the tight ropes.

'I discovered they were using a cove on my land near here to cart barrels of spirits from ships to this mill store and then to sell and avoid paying government tax.'

'But why did they attack you?'

William gave a low moan. 'Because they discovered I was spying on them. They knew I could have them arrested.' She could feel him trying to loosen the knots tying her hands. 'I was naïve not to report them,' he said. 'I should have, but the punishment for smuggling is severe. These men would be hanged or transported, leaving their poor families in dire poverty. I did not want that to happen.'

Jemima had met such families in Dockland with their menfolk in prison. She knew all about that misery and understood William would not want the families to suffer.

'But now you know you have underestimated their ruthlessness.'

It was difficult for William to speak with a split lip, yet he carried on bravely. 'Indeed, I fear I have been negligent, leaving my grandmother to keep an eye on my estates while I was unaware of the extent of the smuggling. I expected them to surrender when I confronted them and offered them a deal, but their leader, Dykes, is a villain.'

Gasping from the effort of speaking, William seemed to have no energy left, and Jemima's tears ran down her face. Her own pain was bad enough — but she felt his too. Angry that he had been beaten up so badly, she suspected he had fought for his life after he had been caught by the smugglers. He must have been easily overpowered — one man against several — and there was no reason to have beaten him. This was unnecessary violence he had suffered.

Why did the local men hurt him?

Until he was old enough to take on the responsibility of the management of the estate, William would have been known to them as a boy. From what Jemima had observed, the estate workers who had accompanied her that night to the mill were in no way surly but wanted to help the young Earl.

William must have been thinking similar thoughts for he said, 'The leader — Dykes — I have discovered controls the other smugglers. He boasted he had killed the maid who had become too nosy about his illegal business and would dispose of me — and them, too.'

Jemima had heard Dykes threaten to kill him too, and knew that although they were prisoners they were lucky to be alive.

Loosening their bonds was slow painful work but the only hope they had of freeing themselves and Jemima continued to bear the pain as William continued worked on the knots that tied her.

Taking a deep breath, William continued, 'Yes, Dykes would have killed me,

I am certain, but the men with him refused to let him. So they tied me up and left me here. He said he would decide what to do with me later. In the meantime they had to go and collect a huge shipment of goods.'

Anxious to keep William from losing consciousness again, Jemima kept him talking.

'Dykes dressed in your clothes. I though he was you when I saw him from a distance. But he is vicious — he hit Peggy.'

'Oh no! Did your maid come with you tonight?'

'Yes, she did. And I am worried about what has happened to her.'

William exclaimed in despair.

Jemima said reassuringly, 'I did not make Peggy come. She came of her own free will. And your grandmother assembled your estate men who came with us too. They are hereabouts . . . I wonder what has happened to them?'

'I am truly sorry I have got you and Peggy into this trap. All I wanted to do was to be able to prove my innocence, but stupidly I have put us all in danger.'

'You are not stupid, William. Your intention was kind, offering the smugglers a reasonable chance to continue with their illegal business in a small way and not to report them. And now you now know who the real villain is,' she said, determined to prevent William from thinking his efforts to clear his name for her sake had all been in vain.

'What use is that if he murders us?'

Jemima remembered the anguish her father suffered when he lost his business in the fire — and how she jollied him up and helped him to overcome his despair after the disaster. She knew she must do the same for William.

She said, 'Dykes has not slaughtered us yet. And don't forget your estate men are near and will surely be looking for us.'

Suddenly, the bonds eased and slipped off Jemima's wrists and she cried out as her stiff arms were released. She was free to move her hands and arms and, despite the aching in her swollen fingers, she began to untie William. It was difficult, but she had no choice but to work at untying the knots until he too was free.

'Oh, Jemima!' William's aching body was reluctant to move, but his will to embrace her overcame his weakness. 'I am so sorry to have put you in this danger.'

She kissed his sore face and gently stroked his matted hair away from his eyes with her fingers.

'It is not your doing, William, as well I know. Dykes has hurt me too. Never even in Dockland have I suffered like this. No man there ever harmed my father or me.' She sighed, and said, 'You have been unlucky to have had a man like him in your employ. Your kindness in allowing the smugglers to get away with their illegal trade only made them become more greedy.'

The joy of being able to put their arms around each other gave them both solace and strength to consider what they could do to get away.

'We cannot stay here,' Jemima said, remembering that Dykes had said he wanted to burn down the mill. William agreed that despite his injuries they had to get away.

As they could hear no sounds of the men in the Mill, William said, 'I expect they are all down at the cove collecting a load of spirits — but they may be back with it at any moment.'

Their need to escape was urgent.

He groaned as he stood, his hand on the wall for support. 'We must find a way out of here, though every movement hurts me.'

Jemima was also aware that his lordship was in his underwear — in much the same state as she had found him in the docks earlier that year.

'Here, put this cloak around you,' she said, reluctant to part with it as it was cold. She went to the door, but as she expected, it was locked.

William was on his feet, tottering

around behind the sacks of flour, and for a moment Jemima feared he had lost his wits.

He exclaimed, 'Ah, here it is!'

She went over to where he stood and saw a small door bolted from the inside which William was trying to unfasten.

'This trapdoor is used when the farmers come with carts of corn to be ground, and to collect bags of flour later. It's not very big. But I was able to crawl through it as a boy, and now I hope we can both ease ourselves out.'

'But we will be caught again.' Jemima was anxious hearing William working at the heavy bolts to ease them open, making them screech.

'Hopefully not, although we must be quick about it while we can hear nothing of the men here.' He sighed with relief as the last of the bolts were eased and the small door creaked open.

If he had not been injured, a fit young man like William would have found it no trouble to ease himself up and out of the hole, but it was a struggle for him. Jemima, who found it difficult enough herself, was conscious of his suffering as she clambered through after him.

The sea air — sharp as the seagull cries — made her inhale in quick gasps. Anxiously looking around her, she saw the early morning was without sunshine and there was a swirling mist.

'At least this fog will hide us,' she said, her teeth chattering in the cold without her cloak.

'That's fine — now come under the cloak with me so you do not freeze to death.'

Momentarily, Jemima thought not of turning into ice, but of her reputation. All her efforts to keep herself from being condemned by Society were of no use. Being obliged to snuggle up under the cloak with a man in his underwear was necessary, but beyond the pale!

But as she was only too glad to feel his warmth, she soon forgot her scruples. She recognised the sense of security of being close to him, as he put his arm around her protectively.

'We shall go this way,' he said, keeping his voice low as if they might be overheard as he guided her footsteps.

William was familiar with the terrain outside the mill, of course, knowing it all his life, and he knew the route the smugglers would take from the beach up to the mill. But as they set off in the opposite direction to try and reach safety, Jemima was hit suddenly by a terrible thought.

She stopped walking, and cried out, 'I cannot go without Peggy!'

# 12

William's voice sounded in her ear, making her quake. 'No, Jemima! We cannot stop and find your maid now. We must not risk getting caught again, or they will surely kill us!'

It seemed as if he had cast off his inexperienced youth and his sufferings had made him a more powerful man. Jemima looked at his bruised, bloodied face and body and tears trickled down her face.

'But William . . . '

'No, Jemima.' He spoke in short gasps. 'We must get away. Before we are discovered. Those smugglers . . . are too dangerous . . . we cannot encounter them again.' He took a deep, pained breath and went on, 'We must get to Tom's house. As fast as we can. It is too risky to try for my house. Or Grandmother's. When Dykes discovers us gone . . . that is where they will search.'

It was hard for Jemima to accept that was the truth of their situation. Although not responsible for her maid being ill-used by the smugglers, she felt the guilt of having brought the girl into danger. She had heard Peggy cry out and knew the poor lass had been struck senseless. Now she was being told she must not try to release her! Haunting her mind was the awful thought that Dykes might have the mill burned down. Jemima wanted to protest again and to tell William to save himself while she hunted for Peggy.

Could she, though? Aching all over and not knowing her whereabouts, would she not be simply walking into more trouble? She looked at William, shivering and grey-faced with pain and shock, and knew she could not leave him. More than that, she knew she loved William and had to help him get away to safety first.

'I wonder what has happened to the estate men who brought us to the mill?'

Jemima muttered as she took his arm as he staggered along.

'They have probably gone after the smugglers, thinking we are with them.'

It seemed likely they would have, so Jemima went along with William's directions when he said, 'We must get down to the river bank. Take my rowing boat to Tom Corbishire's manor house.'

It was a sensible plan, but hard for Jemima to accept, knowing she had to leave Peggy tied up somewhere in the mill. Or was she already dead? Jemima shuddered, not liking to think what could have happened to her poor little maid. The urgency of their need to escape came back into her mind, and she would have enough to do helping William with his injuries, she would not be able to assist Peggy at the same time, so she refrained from arguing.

Although she felt shaky and pained, she felt sure William was in a far worse state than herself. Indeed, he was gasping, obviously having difficulty speaking and moving, and she resolved not to delay him reaching safety.

She allowed him to guide her along a pathway he seemed to know. Bushes hid them, although the rustling leaves as they brushed past made Jemima jumpy as they could be discovered by smugglers if any were around.

They plodded on to where the path ended and there she saw the river gleaming like silver — and coming nearer she saw on the riverbank a small boathouse and landing stage.

'This is one of my sailing boats,' William said, with a hint of pride. 'I keep it here in the summer. To sail alone . . . when I get time . . . away from my estate duties.'

That was something she had learned about him — the life's work he had inherited of looking after his estate, but his recreation was his love of sailing.

The physical effort of getting the boat out of the boathouse and getting themselves into it was going to be another difficulty.

'I hope we are not discovered before

we can get away.' He voiced the concern of them both as the morning light became stronger.

He insisted Jemima be covered with the cloak, assuring her he no longer required it as the exertion of rowing would soon warm him. He had the greatest difficulty untying the boat and easing it out onto the river, then getting himself into the boat, which lurched alarmingly on the water.

'Step in,' he told Jemima, who hesitated seeing the boat rock violently from side to side.

The water was deep, and she could not swim.

'Come along!' he ordered.

She was afraid to step forward with nothing to hold on to. A hollered voice made her freeze. Out of the mist a man came running towards them — then another following him.

Jemima gulped in terror. They had been caught! Terrified, she jumped into the boat — and fell over.

She heard one of the men exclaim,

'Zounds, if it 'ain't his lordship with his lady!'

Open-mouthed Jemima gaped to find two footmen in livery staring at them, as amazed to see her as she them.

Relief flooded her! They were not their enemies but household servants who had been sent out to find them.

William's wild appearance had the effect of making the servants goggle-eyed and dumb.

'Don't just stand there — help us,' William cried out.

The older man said, 'Yes, my lord,' but seemed unable to know what he should do, and continued to stand on the riverbank and stare at the earl's nearly undressed and battered state.

'His lordship wants you to get into the boat and row us upriver to Mr Corbishire's manor,' said Jemima, finding her voice after the fright she had had.

The two men looked at each other and shook their heads. 'We can't row a boat, ma'am.'

'Just get in. I'll teach you,' William gasped, holding his arms wrapped around his aching ribs.

Partly because they could see their lord in great pain and wanted to help him, and partly because they could not get him out of the boat from the bank, the two men gingerly stepped into the boat — which rocked violently and almost toppled the craft over. Water slopped into the boat as it lurched from side to side.

'Sit down!' yelled William.

The situation became almost comical, even to Jemima, although she was terrified of falling into the water. Even she could tell the boat was overloaded, and had sunk lower into the water. But she knew William would not have told the men to get in unless he knew it could take the weight, and he badly needed their assistance.

Nevertheless, she felt alarmed as they untied the boat and sailed away from the mooring.

Jemima shook herself; being negative

and afraid would not help matters. William would know of such danger.

Despite obviously having difficulty in controlling his traumatised mind and body, it was clear William had to take charge of sailing the boat as the two footmen were unable to. With instructions from him, the two men sat and found the oars and, with a lot of splashing which drenched them all, eventually turned the boat and managed, with great difficulty because of the tidal flow, to start rowing upriver.

In between his exclamations of pain and cold, William struggled to tell them how to proceed. Jemima could do nothing to assist. She was a city girl and could not row a boat.

'Oh!' Jemima cried out, alarmed. A heron, disturbed by them, flapped its wide wings as it flew over her. Even though she was still afraid, she was enchanted by the early morning sights and sounds of nature — swimming otters and bird calls — as they floated by water meadows and grazing cattle.

What seemed like ages of agony was finally ended when another craft came in sight.

'Ahoy!' yelled William to the men in the boats who were fishing. Jemima relaxed, knowing they were not the smugglers, or William would not have hailed them.

The fishermen came alongside and, after seeing and hearing who was in the boat, immediately offered assistance. A rope was fastened to tug them closer as they helped the exhausted Earl, assuring him that he would be taken upriver to Tom's manor.

Almost fainting herself, Jemima was barely conscious of being carried off the boat a little later, and taken to the manor house. She was only dimly aware of people anxious to help them, and being assisted upstairs, and placed in a bed heated with a brass bed warmer.

Surrounded by a bevy of maids who came to assist her, Jemima knew William would be also well looked after, and soon fell asleep.

It was like coming out of a bad dream. Jemima realised the nightmare was over and she was safely cosseted in a warm bed — although her body soon reminded her of its aches and pains after her ordeal the night before, as she tried to move her body.

'How is she, Doctor?'

Jemima saw several people around her, and heard voices she recognised.

Mary Corbishire was looking over her anxiously, and the Dowager Lady Swanington was in the room talking to a gentleman whom Jemima presumed was the doctor.

'The young lady is not about to fade away, your ladyship. All she needs — apart from the healing salves — is rest and some breakfast.'

Jemima smiled. The doctor was right. She had suffered many uncomfortable times as a poor woman in Gin Lane, but she was basically healthy. Her sore arms and wrists she knew would heal.

She raised herself to ask, 'How is William?'

The countess came to sit on a chair by her bed. 'Once again, you have saved him, my dear,' she said. 'And I cannot thank you enough.'

Pleased to know William was saved, yet still wondering how he was, as he had been hurt far worse that she had been, she asked anxiously, 'Is he recovering from his injuries, ma'am?'

'Why, yes.' The doctor came over and reassured her. 'The Earl of Swanington is a young man. He will rally — in time.' The doctor smiled at her. 'Although he may not look quite as handsome as he was before he was beaten up.'

Jemima pictured his lordship's cut and bruised face, and expected his body may have scars too. She enquired, 'Is he . . . has he suffered any serious wounds?'

The doctor looked sympathetically into Jemima's fearful eyes saying, 'A broken rib or two, which will be painful for him, but there is nothing more than superficial wounds. He should recover well in time, with good nursing.'

'I can nurse him, Doctor,' Jemima replied. 'I nursed my father before he died.'

The silence that resulted after her statement quickly reminded Jemima that as un unmarried woman she should not have offered to do something as personal as tending a man.

Lady Swanington intervened, 'Quite so, my dear, but there are servants here to look after him.' She smiled and took Jemima's hand. 'I think all William needs from you is companionship.' The old lady turned to Mary Corbishire and asked, 'May I suggest Miss Perrot stays here for while?'

Mary nodded. 'Of course she is welcome to stay here, your ladyship.'

Jemima lay back on her pillows and smiled at the two kind ladies. However, she was concerned that her relationship with William might be altered after his ordeal. Was he suffering from something they were unwilling to tell her about?

Mary said, 'We will leave you to rest now. I shall see that the maid brings you some breakfast.'

As they left the room, Jemima felt blessed to have two ladies who cared about her as they cared for William.

The doctor, although he had assured her that William was not in grave danger, had hinted that he might be a changed man after his ordeal. Jemima hoped William would resume his estate duties with a ruthless determination to stamp out the corruption that had been going on behind his back. She wondered if Dykes and his gang were in Exeter jail now. She would be sure to ask about that when she got up.

★ ★ ★

A little later, drinking coffee and eating a late breakfast of coddled eggs and muffins, Jemima realised she had not enquired about Peggy. Smitten with guilt that she had neglected to ask about her maid's welfare, Jemima almost jumped out of bed to ring the bell-pull. But she did not have to as just then, a maid knocked and came into collect her breakfast tray.

'Have the smugglers been caught? Has Peggy been released?' Jemima asked, breathlessly.

'I don't know nothing 'bout them, ma'am,' replied the maid. 'I'll ask when I go downstairs.'

It was tantalising to have to wait, but it was her own fault for not thinking of it earlier. Now there was nothing she could do but wait and hope.

Before long other maids appeared and carried in a bath tub and jugs of hot water for her to bathe, and an array of soothing herbal ointments for her wounds.

'Lovely!' breathed Jemima as a screen was put around her and she was able to step into the sweet-smelling water and relax in the tub. But at the back of her mind, she was more concerned to know the outcome of the search for the smugglers and to know how Peggy was.

The black-dressed housekeeper came in to see that their visitor had all she needed and wanted, and remarked, 'I understand there was a deal of activity down by the coast last night. The constables have made many arrests.'

Jemima sloshed water over the side of the bath as she sat up quickly.

'Is there any news of Peggy, my maid?'

'I understand your maid returned to the Dower House and is there now.'

Jemima felt immediately relieved to hear that news. 'Was she badly hurt?' she asked before taking a deep breath as a maid poured a jug full of warm water over her head.

The housekeeper had brought clothes for Jemima and was sorting them out and instructing the maids on the salves and bandages to put on Jemima's injured wrists.

She replied, 'I heard your maid is a tough young woman, ma'am. I believe they had trouble understanding her Cockney accent, as she was very frightened and gabbling, but eventually they understood what she said about the smugglers so the estate men could go and catch them.

'Then she was upset because she did not know what had happened to you and his lordship when you were not found. She thought you had been taken to the beach by the smugglers to collect the booty they were expecting last night. That's why the estate men did not go and search the mill for you earlier.'

As Jemima's wrists were being soothed with ointment, she thought what a muddle it had all been last night! But it was now becoming clear to her what had happened.

She asked, 'Did Peggy say how she had escaped?'

'She said she had scarpered — made a run for it, we think she meant.'

Jemima chuckled, understanding the Cockney slang. Getting out of the bath, Jemima felt refreshed. She would question Peggy about her escape later.

Her hair was patted dry with towels, then combed and dressed, and she was assisted to slip on some clean under-wear and a morning gown. It made her look and feel like a young lady again. She thanked everyone who helped her.

'It is a pleasure to dress such a pretty young lady,' said one maid with a smile and a bob, as she stood back to see the transformation that had been made on the bedraggled girl who had been brought to the manor in the early morning.

Jemima was now well rested, and one of her first tasks was to find out how William would regard her. Did he really need her, as his grandmother had said? Or would she go back to London to her home with her brother, Charles?

If so, she would live life as a spinster, because she knew she could never love any other man.

# 13

Later that day, although yearning to see William, Jemima feared what she might learn about his condition as she sat with Mary on the sofa in their parlour before dinner. How permanently badly hurt was he?

When Tom came downstairs from William's sick room and announced to his sister Mary, and his guest Jemima, that the patient, 'had no desire to see the ladies,' Jemima's face fell.

Disappointed he did not want to see her, Jemima enquired, 'Tom, I was wondering . . . well, please tell me *exactly*, how William is.'

Tom's leather shoes clomped over the floorboards as he paced the room, as if deciding what to say. At last he replied, 'I must admit William is not quite himself, which is not surprising after the bruising he received!'

'How has he changed?' Jemima frowned as she rubbed her fingers together nervously.

Mary looked at Jemima sympathetically and said, 'I am certain he just needs time to recover.'

'A long time, I should think,' Tom retorted.

Jemima was still none the wiser as to what was ailing William. 'Tom, please tell me what you think is the matter with him. You know his lordship and I are well acquainted.'

'Yes, yes, we do know. Mary and I have known for some time how he admires you, Jemima.'

'He loves you,' corrected Mary, taking Jemima's hand to comfort her.

Flushing, Jemima turned to look out of the parlour window. She could not deny their love, neither did she want to, but was that love now in the past? She said, 'It is because I love William that I want to know how I can help him. It is obvious to me that there has been a change in him. I was not there when the

217

smugglers attacked him. I found him tied up and injured. Then in the gloom of the early morning we managed to escape from the storeroom where we had been locked in . . . '

Jemima gave a shudder, remembering the danger of situation before she could continue.

'We were both terrified, struggling to get away before the smugglers came back.'

'Yes, indeed,' Tom said, standing before Jemima, 'William told me that no other young lady could have saved him as you did.'

Knowing women brought up in poverty in dockland, Jemima could think of many who would have had the strength to assist him and retorted, 'Oh, I'm sure they would, if they had to!'

Mary said seriously, 'No, Jemima. You, like your maid Peggy, have had much hardship to bear in your life, and your determination to overcome your misfortune, and cheerfulness in helping others in trouble, has given you an advantage over most young ladies who have never had to put up with more than pricking their finger on a sewing needle.'

Jemima smiled — then became anxious again.

'Dear friends, the question is, how can I assist William now? I am at a loss to know what it is about him that you are hiding from me.'

Brother and sister looked at each other.

Tom cleared his throat. 'Be patient, Jemima.'

Mary smartly interrupted with, 'Is that the gong I hear for dinner being served?'

Jemima rose with Mary and walked alongside her into the dining room, thinking rather sadly that she would just have to wait to assess William's condition herself. That was, of course, when she was allowed to see him.

Perhaps it was William who was refusing to see her? Why was that? Was he now ashamed of his appearance?

The next day, after another good night's rest, Jemima felt very much better, even still with sore arms and wrists to remind her of her horrendous night's adventure.

As the maid brushed her hair and began to dress it becomingly, she looked at herself in the dressing mirror and reflected. Was she able to be the kind of companion for her grandson that Lady Swanington had in mind? Did she want to be a companion to an earl anyway? Perhaps she should accept that whatever had happened to William, it had made him change his mind about wanting to marry her?

Did she still want to marry him? To live in his great house with so many rooms and servants? She had liked her simple life in London, living in a comfortable though modest house with her Cockney servants, helping Charles with his shop and having Sylvia's jolly companionship.

She shook her head. Of course she wanted to be with William. Her heart told her, her body longed for his embrace. She would never be happy if she refused to stay and be William's companion, as his grandmother had suggested. She would be unfulfilled as a woman and if she left him now, they would both ache for each other.

At least now she knew she must stay a while and see how things were between them.

'Do you know how his lordship is this morning?' she asked the maid who had come to help her dress, hoping that hearing the servant's gossip would enlighten her.

'I heard he was in a fine temper this morning.'

'Is he being a bother in the household?'

The maid nodded as she slipped a pretty muslin gown over Jemima's head and fastened the row of small buttons down the back.

'You could say that, ma'am.'

'In what way?'

'I suppose I shouldn't say it, you being a guest here and all, but since he's been here everything's been upside down.'

'Goodness me! In what way?'

The maid looked over her shoulder hurriedly as if she did not want to be overheard.

'Mr Tom and his lordship shout at each other now, but they used to be friends.'

Jemima asked, 'Do you know why?'

'I don't, ma'am, no.' The maid went on in a whisper, 'But Miss Mary has trouble with him too. He throws things about and the maids have to clear it up. He says he cannot even dress himself properly because his valet is missing. And worst of all his language is . . . well . . . '

'Why do they not move him to Swanington Hall?' Jemima asked.

'I think it is because he is still injured and needs nursing.'

Jemima thought about it and said, 'I

gather he is being a difficult patient?'

The maid nodded, 'Yes, ma'am. I would say that was true.'

Alarmed to hear of the Earl's bad behaviour, Jemima sighed. She had always thought of him as being very controlled in his manners, very gentlemanly, and not at all the kind of petulant man she was hearing him being described as.

There was no doubt in Jemima's mind that William was a powerful man, not only because of the wealth and the position he had been born to, but also because his physical and mental abilities were sound — apart from his present injuries, but the doctor had told her he would recover. And in the past he had suffered as a youngster growing up without his parents to guide him. That experience must have had an effect on him — as suffering had also taught her.

However, suffering and disasters in one's life could make one petty and vindictive. Or they could bring wisdom.

Jemima had, she hoped, chosen to develop from the innocent girl she used to be — like her delightful friend, Sylvia — to become a mature woman after her experiences. William would need to do the same, or he would become a disgruntled nobleman shut up in his grand hall for the rest of his life. His wise grandmother recognised that possibility, and that was no doubt why she had asked her to help him.

Armed with some understanding of the problem she faced, Jemima went down to breakfast. Mary was at the breakfast table and greeted Jemima warmly.

'How are you this morning, Jemima?'

'Considerably better, thank you.'

Mary poured her some coffee saying, 'The breakfast dishes are on the sideboard, if you would care to help yourself.'

Seeing the array of bacon, eggs, kidneys, kippers, haddock, and hot muffins to choose from, Jemima almost laughed.

'My goodness — you do intend to feed me up!'

'Yes I do,' retorted Mary. 'Girls in love tend to lose weight and you are becoming dangerously thin, and besides, I want you to gain strength as I was hoping you would accompany me shopping this morning. It is a long carriage drive into Exeter, but a shopping trip is fun, if exhausting.'

Jemima agreed. She felt she needed some new clothes to suit her new situation.

Nevertheless, she said, 'I must see William before we go.' Mary's silence made Jemima add, 'I know he says he does not want to see me, but I am aware that his lordship is behaving like a grumpy grizzly bear!'

Mary's wide eyes showed she was surprised, but she nodded agreement.

'If I am to consider marriage with William, I have to know the worst as well as the best about him, Mary. And I am not unused to dealing with men's unsavoury characteristics.'

Mary looked at Jemima sympatheti-cally.

'Tom has often asked me why I do not show an interest in William myself. I have known him since we were young, but I see William as a man I like but could not cope with. I looked for a more gentle man to marry. I agree with the Countess that William needs a strong woman, like you.'

Jemima did not like the idea of being called a 'strong woman'. No, she was an ordinary woman with feminine charac-teristics of being physically weaker than a man, with a soft body and hopefully the gracious manners of a lady.

'Mary, I do not know that I can manage the wild man you describe he has become!'

'Oh, yes you can, Jemima. Tom and I think you are just the right lady for him. And William knows it too. We must hope he will soon overcome his present rage! In the meantime, let us forget him until his mood improves. We shall think about the pretty bonnets and shoes to

226

be bought in the shops in Exeter.'

Jemima smiled. How delightful it would to be have additions to her wardrobe, but she said, 'New hats and shoes for me will have to wait a while. First I must venture into the wild beast's cage and tame him!'

Mary gasped, no doubt thinking that a lady going into a man's bedchamber was simply not done! But her expression changed as Jemima said, 'Be not alarmed, Mary. I am not afraid of William, in a foul temper or not.'

Mary's expression showed she was uncertain, but she gave Jemima a slight smile and said, 'Well, I suppose you can visit him as he is unwell — and there is a certain amount of, em . . . agreement between you, is there not?'

Jemima, smiled ruefully saying, 'That is precisely what I must find out.'

Mary wagged her finger at Jemima. 'You must not let him eat you! I shall get a manservant to accompany you.'

'Very well, if it will reassure you.'

'And let me remind you that we must

leave for town by ten this morning or we shall never get home before dark.'

Jemima calmly helped herself to some coddled eggs and bacon and sat down to eat, thinking she ought to fortify herself against the brickbats she might get when visiting William.

'Oh, I shan't take long putting William in order,' she said with a smile.

Mary looked at her disbelievingly. She said, 'Please be careful, Jemima. I will call for a footman to make sure William has finished his ablutions, and then have him escort you to his rooms when you have finished your breakfast.'

Jemima felt determined that whatever physical state she found William in, she would not be bullied. Eating breakfast, she said, 'If he is unbearable I shall tell him so. One way or another he shall hear what I have to say!'

Mary laughed. 'I admire your courage. William in a temper is too much for me! But however badly he behaves, you shall have a pleasant day looking around the delightful shops in Exeter to look forward too.'

A nagging thought spoiled Jemima's breakfast — that she had to find out if William had an uncontrollable temper at other times. Could she marry a man who had that characteristic?

A little later, having prepared herself with a second cup of coffee, Jemima left the civilised company of Mary in the breakfast room, and followed a manservant up the manor's grand staircase and along a wide corridor with windows looking out over the green lawns and flower gardens. Then she heard a man shouting.

Jemima pursed her lips, guessing who was causing the rumpus.

They arrived at William's mahogany bedroom door. The servant knocked on it politely. Hearing no reply, the servant tapped again, putting his ear against the door waiting for the sound of a voice to tell him to enter. Still hearing nothing, the servant knocked again more loudly.

Suddenly the door swung open and Jemima stepped backwards, mouth ajar in surprise and alarm to see the powerful Earl of Swanington standing before her in his nightshirt.

'Don't scratch away at the door like a mouse, man!' bellowed William.

Then noticing Jemima, it was his turn to look amazed as he stared at her.

'Jemima! Miss Perrot, I had no idea . . .'

Jemima looked up at his injured face and blazing eyes as she gathered her wits.

'I do not suppose you expected me, my lord, but that does not give you the excuse to be ill-mannered. Now let me in. I wish to talk to you.'

He looked aghast. 'I'm not dressed.'

'I can see that! And that is not the worst of it. You are acting like a Gin Lane drunkard!'

She was pleased to note he looked a little shamefaced.

'I am unwell,' he muttered.

Seeing the wounds on his face she had to agree he had lost some of his perfect good looks, but the battle scars had given him a strangely attractive manly maturity — he had become even more physically desirable in her eyes.

William was studying her too.

'The main thing wrong with you, William,' she snapped, 'Is your attitude. You are behaving with no thought for others, upsetting your kind host and hostess and frightening their servants. It is quite disgraceful of you. *And* you need to comb you hair and shave.'

He gulped visibly and Jemima felt she had made a good start.

Aware the servant had gone, she attempted to enter his room. 'Now let me come in and speak with you properly.'

William's arm shot out to bar the doorway as he said, 'It would not be proper.'

Jemima replied, 'My goodness, William. It is a little late for you to be considering what is correct and what is not! Especially after the way you have been causing chaos in your friend's house. If Tom and Mary were not better friends they would have shipped you off to Swanington Hall to sulk alone!'

He opened his mouth to say something but closed it again.

Jemima said, more softly this time, 'Now, am I to stand in the corridor to discuss our future, or are you going to allow me to enter?'

He hesitated, and Jemima felt sorry for him as she suddenly realised he was not only bearing scars she could see, but seemed to be deeply hurt inside, too — and that his blustering had been hiding real distress. But what could it be?

Stepping aside, he allowed Jemima to enter.

The nobleman's wardrobe accessories were scattered everywhere. Obviously he had had some of his things brought over from Swanington Hall. There was a trunk load of clothes open to reveal piles of underwear and various sized boxes containing his personal items.

Everything a well-dressed man could possibly need, from leather boots in shoe stretchers to boxes with toilet items, suits and shirts nicely pressed, to leather gloves and even an umbrella! All his things should have been stored away in his dressing-room, not left about untidily.

'Goodness me, William!' Jemima exclaimed, her practised eye used to assessing the value of gentleman's quality items in the pawn shop. 'You should be content. Is there anything else on earth you could possibly want?'

He glowered at her.

'Obviously, there is,' Jemima declared crossly looking around in vain for space to sit. Failing to find anywhere, she stood and faced the disgruntled earl. 'Be quick telling me about it because I am to go shopping with Mary and she says we must leave by ten.'

Seeing the fury on his face, Jemima realised she had probably overstepped the mark — he looked as if he would roar at her any moment! She braced herself for the onslaught, thinking she could always run away down the corridor. But, suddenly he turned, stepped over some of the boxes and clutter, and sat down on his bed lowering his head and looking defeated.

'I am sorry about this mess. I need my valet.'

Jemima immediately remembered Dykes, and considered it the wrong time to offer him condolences about his former servant — who she thought would now be languishing in jail, and deservingly so.

Instead, she looked again around the room and said, 'I should think you do! I am sure there are plenty of servants who would be pleased to dress you and look after your wardrobe.'

'But who can I trust? My estate workers have been found to be ruthless smugglers!'

'Not all of them, William. You know Dykes, as ringleader, threatened many of them to join him.'

'Yes, but he might well have killed me. You told me they planned to burn the mill — with us in it!'

Jemima shuddered to think of the

danger they were in last night, and was it not impossible, as earl of a great estate, that he had other enemies, and that there were other villains living on his land? She asked, 'Can Tom not select a suitable manservant for you?'

'I really do not know.'

Jemima began to understand the earl's dilemma. He had been badly let down, betrayed by Dykes. He had grown up surrounded by employees he had always felt respected him as he had always tried to be fair to them, but now he realised he could not tell after last night which of them might thrust a knife in him. He felt under threat on his own estate.

She saw his plight because she knew that feeling of uncertainty. She had been wary of him, even though she loved him. She had refused to marry William the first time and even the second time he had asked her, because there was a lingering doubt in her mind about his innocence and integrity.

Was he not now in the same boat?

Wondering if he could ever totally trust even his closest servants again. How could she console him?

'William,' she said gently, 'I do have sympathy with your anger over being betrayed by Dykes, but your happiness — and mine — will not be achieved if you persist in allowing that evil man to prevent you from moving on. After all, Dykes will be hanged for murder. You should try to forget him.'

The anguished wail of pain from William made Jemima start.

'How can I possibly move on when he is free to roam — and may strike me again at any moment?'

# 14

Upset and angry to hear William talking like that, Jemima looked at him with a puzzled expression. Had his beating affected his head and made him somewhat witless?

'What do you mean that Dykes is free to roam? He is in prison, is he not?'

William removed one of his slippers and threw it with force to the other side of the room. It slammed against the wall and slid to the ground, as he cried, 'No! My estate men failed to catch the slippery villain! And there are not enough constables in this area to track him down.'

'Oh, no!' Jemima gasped. It could not be . . . or was it true? She looked at William who sat once more with his head downcast, looking defeated.

After her initial shock at hearing the dreadful news, Jemima walked over and sat beside him, putting her arm around

William's drooping shoulders.

'I am truly sorry to hear it,' she said.

His tense body told her of his fury.

She had been mistaken about him being defeated — downcast yes, indeed he was — but it was not petulance. Rather, he was like a coiled snake ready to strike, frustrated, feeling powerless to know what to do.

'Tom is out hunting for Dykes — he and the few men who are with him — but Tom will not allow me to go with him, even though I know the estate better than he does . . . ' William's voice quavered and petered out.

'Tom is only worried you are not well enough for too much exertion yet, William.'

'But that wretched man is having time to go underground while I am kept here.'

She sighed. What could she do to ease his mental anguish? She felt to hold his strong hand which gripped hers so tightiy that she almost exclaimed for him to release her.

'I know you are capable of overcoming a criminal like Dykes. But now you know who killed your maid and has harmed others, including yourself, your quarry is a marked man, so your suffering has not been in vain. Your target is clear which it was not before.'

'But I have no idea where is now.'

'Please . . . you are crushing my hand . . . '

'Oh! I am sorry!'

He released his tight grip and taking her hand, lifted it to kiss it gently on the sensitive part of the underside of her wrist.

Thrilled at the sensation his kiss gave her, yet remembering why she had come to see him, she said, 'I am certain that together we can think of a way to catch Dykes.'

He chuckled. 'Oh, Jemima, most of my estate workers are out searching for him — how can a young lady like you do better than they can?'

'Well, if they find him, that is all well and good. But if they cannot . . . '

She felt his arm easing her towards him so he could hold her body. She felt he needed her to comfort him and she wanted to ease his pain if she could. Their eyes met and held in mutual understanding. He cupped her chin and gently raised her face so that he could kiss her.

Feeling his lips on hers Jemima forgot everything and allowed their passion for each other to indulge in a lingering kiss.

They did not have to say anything after that for a while — both knew the danger they were in. The evil man, who had already expressed the desire to kill the earl, was in hiding somewhere and was a threat to them. Dykes was clever, able to influence others as he pleased. He might opt to go abroad or stalk them for days, months, or even years.

Jemima's hands, which she had slipped around William's neck, she removed, suddenly aware anyone could observe them with the door wide open.

She had to think of a solution to the

earl's problem. For it was his — she could escape back to London at any time. He was stuck here at Swanington. It was his home, and he and his grandmother, who had done so much for him, who needed to be able to live in peace without a madman at their heels.

'We both know Dykes must be caught,' she said. 'And you must believe you will get him eventually.'

William seemed to be revived by her show of love and support for him.

'You are right,' he said. 'But how can I find him — let alone trap him?'

Jemima suddenly remembered Mary would be waiting for her. 'I must go now,' she said, 'but despair not, for I think I know how Dykes can be tracked down. There are many so-called villains in Gin Lane who would be only too pleased to go manhunting for you — if you pay them well enough. You know the saying: use a thief to catch a thief. Besides, some owe you for stealing the money you were going to take abroad a few months ago.'

William brightened. 'If they will come, I shall make it worth their while.'

'Good. Then I shall send an express letter to Charles to ask him to collect some men from Gin Lane to search for Dykes. But, remember they are thieves so you will have to warn your butler to put your silver under lock and key — and warn your retainers to count their chickens!'

Jemima was delighted to see him laugh.

'I shall promise to reimburse them any losses.'

Jemima was pleased to see him look relieved to hear a way out of his dilemma. She added, 'Now please, out of politeness to your kind friends, Mary and Tom, put aside your gloom and return to being a man of good manners. Your grandmother has asked me to stay here, as your friend.'

She rose to leave the room, but not before hearing him call after her, 'You are more to me than just a friend . . . bless you, Jemima.'

Sitting beside Mary in the small carriage going towards Exeter, with their maid sitting with the carriage driver in front, Jemima quietly told her about the problem William was suffering from.

'He is angry to have been caught up in the scandal of the maid's death, as well as the injuries he has been dealt from his evil valet. But he worries too because Dykes is still free, and he has not the men who can be spared from their normal work to capture him. I suppose he will need to recruit more.'

Mary listened sympathetically as Jemima explained further, 'I must go to the Post Office as soon as we arrive and send a letter by express to Charles. I am certain that Blind Joe will seek out some ruffians in the Dockland, who will be willing to come here and assist in the search for Dykes. Charles, I hope, will organise a large cart to bring them from London to Swanington as soon possible.'

Mary nodded but said, 'And as soon as you have finished in the Post Office, my dear, you are to put aside your troubles and enjoy yourself.'

That Jemima determined to do as soon as they arrived in the charming old town of Exeter. They went straight to the Post Office, where Jemima wrote the letter and posted it.

Jemima appreciated Mary's bubbly enthusiasm — just as she enjoyed her friend, Sylvia's company. If she were to marry William, she was thrilled to know that Mary would be her friend and neighbour, just as Tom was William's.

# 15

The Dowager Countess kissed Jemima's cheek and said, 'I could not have chosen a better bride for my grandson than you, my dear. I had the strong feeling ever since I heard of your bravery in rescuing him in London, that you were the right woman for William.'

'Thank you,' murmured Jemima

The countess continued, 'My only wish now is that you shall both enjoy the privileges you have been given.'

Jemima felt her new situation was both thrilling and daunting. In her heart she felt it right for her to prepare to marry the man she had chosen since she had first set eyes on him. The fact that he was a nobleman seemed more of a nuisance than the pleasure it might seem to most young women who dreamed of capturing the heart of a gentleman high in Society. Jemima had never thought along those lines — only to marry a man she loved and who loved her. But her love affair was the way it had happened — by accident.

It was a time to rejoice and yet she knew both she and William had a shadow over them that had to be removed — an unresolved murder.

Unfortunately, used to being independent, the social shackles she found herself in irked her. She did not appreciate the lack of privacy and decided she must speak to William about it.

Even trying to see him in private was not easy. His joy at finding the woman he wanted to marry had given him added confidence, and he strode around his estate overseeing what had to be done to improve and maintain it. The estate workers and villagers liked to see the tall, handsome young earl, and appreciated his concern for their jobs and welfare. They knew his life had been in danger by the fugitive smuggler and murderer, Dykes, and that his lordship was even now hunting him down. Many had suggestions as to where the villain was hiding and William was sent on many a false trail to find him. It all took up so much of his time.

The Earl had to attend the trial of Dykes's smugglers, who had been caught, and he persuaded the magistrate to show mercy to those with families to support — but as they had broken the law he could only arrange for their families to be given assistance. Feeling dejected as he rode back from the trial, William felt determined to keep a tight rein on his employees so that no more got into trouble with the law.

Jemima and Peggy had made full use of the purchases made in Exeter. Jemima's appearance in her dinner gown took William's breath away. No woman could have looked lovelier than his intended bride that evening. Her naturally lithe body was enhanced by the quality of her high waisted, cream muslin gown, the simplicity of the garment adorned by the jewellery he had gifted her. The necklace he had chosen for her seemed to make her belong to him.

Her hair was swept up expertly — Peggy had been taught by another lady's maid to do so — which gave her grace and allowed him to admire the soft skin of her neck and shoulders and the low decolletage of her gown. Even her neat evening slippers enticed him to want to kiss them!

The dining room with its circular dining table made for a more intimate family meal, and Mr Sprott, the butler, oversaw the smooth running of the food the maids brought in from the kitchen.

'You look wearied, William,' remarked the countess.

William hid a yawn. 'Yes, I am somewhat.'

The candelabrum flickered light onto his strained face as Jemima asked, 'You attended the smugglers trial today, did you not?' As he continued to eat his fish, she added, 'Will you tell us what happened?'

The clattering of his knife and fork onto his plate jarred the pleasure of the meal.

'No, Jemima, I shall not discuss over dinner what I think of the British justice system, nor my private affairs.'

Rebuked, Jemima held her temper. She was used to eating and talking to her companions about the daily happenings, good or bad, during a meal together. Even her late father and brother would discuss their business over a family meal.

Picking up her long-stemmed wine glass, she sipped a few times, and then said, 'You must forgive my ill manners, for I am used to being able to say what is on my mind.'

The countess nodded. 'Quite right too.'

William looked ready to tear his table napkin from his lap, throw it onto the table and stalk out of the room — only his grandmother fixed her eyes on him with such a glare he seemed to think better of it. He continued eating as if he did not really care for the food.

*So this is life in high society,* thought Jemima. *Governed by rules about what one should and should not do.* She continued eating in silence, listening to the countess tactfully making conversation of no consequence.

Of course, William was right. Whatever had happened at the Assizes was bound to be sad — local families whose relatives had joined Dykes in illegal smuggling and had been punished, would be in anguish. She should have thought of that.

It was quite strange to think that only a year ago she was one of the lowest working women in London, sharing a meal of sausage with a poor blind man and his dog.

The dramatic change was not entirely to her liking, but she loved William, and he could not change his position as an Earl, nor his problem about finding his villainous former valet. She had to make the best of both the good and bad of her situation.

The happiness of being in love, of seeing the Dowager Countess so overjoyed to learn of her acceptance of William's proposal of marriage, and knowing the grand lady's belief that she would make William a good wife, was very pleasing to her.

When she had told her maid, Peggy, she was full of chat about what the other servants said about her marrying the Earl.

'Lordy, miss, they were that pleased when they was told. Drank to your 'ealth, they did. Said they was looking forward to 'aving some children runnin' around the place.'

Mildly shocked to think that the servants should be thinking of not only of her wedding but of future christenings too, Jemima coloured. As William had warned her, her private life would no longer be entirely private. But, of course, she was delighted to know she had been accepted.

Not entirely though . . .

William's bad humour was later explained by his announcement that he had received some new news that did not please him. After dinner, when they had retired to the privacy of the countess's elegant saloon for coffee, without servants to overhear, he told the ladies that some of his distant relatives — including the heir to his title — were not pleased to learn of his engagement. And they intended to visit the Earl of Swanington, presumably to dissuade him from his intended marriage to a woman of questionable standing in Society, hinting that Jemima was a gold digger from the gutter!

Of course, William was careful not to repeat those words his Aunt Josephina had written but only the gist of what she and her husband, Augustus, thought about his intended bride.

The countess, seated on the settee beside Jemima, sighed on hearing of their intended visit.

'I am afraid the late earl's sister, Lady

Josephina, has always been a thorn in my side, Jemima. As a bride, I too was considered not good enough.' She looked at Jemima, her head sympathetically on one side. 'I have no doubt she will do her best to unseat you, my dear. She quite wrongly thinks that Swanington was destined for her son, Clarence, after her brother died.

'The fact that William is the rightful earl and no longer a small boy she can manipulate — or prevent from marrying — does not seem to have occurred to her. But she is intent on upsetting us with a visit, with her husband and son, nevertheless.'

Jemima swallowed. A murderous valet running around — and now a trio of unpleasant relatives to cope with! Why she thought the situation amusing was because she had some news of her own.

'Now I must tell you my news,' she said, smiling gently.

The countess and William looked at her keenly.

'My brother Charles has replied to my letter. He is, as you know, a much-travelled gentleman used to dealing with various types of people. He tells me he has approached Blind Joe Bundy and suggested he might be able to assemble some men from Dockland to come to Swanington for a camping holiday. To hunt for Dykes. That is, if you would like them to because, as I explained, they will be a noisy crowd of vagabonds. I cannot see your relatives and my disreputable London guests getting along well.'

William, Jemima was relieved to see, chuckled.

'We cannot stop Aunt Josephina from coming to Swanington, if she has made up her mind. She is like a tempest approaching. Nor can we delay our search for Dykes — we have already exhausted ourselves trying to find him, and the men must start bringing in the harvest.' He frowned and gave a long sigh. 'I am in a fix! What do you think of the Londoners being here to help in the search, Grandmama?'

The countess looked a little surprised, but said, 'William, I am no longer your guardian — you must decide this matter yourself.'

The earl, who was seated in a relaxed manner on one of the fine Chippendale carved chairs in the saloon, looked splendid in his evening dress. Jemima's eyes could only remain looking admiringly at the handsome man she loved. With his elbows resting on the arms of the chair and his well-shaped hands together as if in prayer under his chin, he was reflecting, not shirking his duty to take the responsibility he was born to and his grandmother had striven to prepare him for.

Jemima knew William to be an honourable man, albeit with a temper at times. He was responsible for the welfare of the residents in his great house and on his estates. She knew he must be weighing up the pros and cons. Was he prepared to allow a horde of vagabonds loose all over Swanington, in the hope that they might capture the elusive Dykes?

'Well,' he said at last, like a statue coming alive, 'if you ladies do not object, I think Jemima's acquaintances are probably going to be the only way in which Dykes can be found and captured. Unless the evil man has already skipped abroad from one of the seaports.' He gave a hollow laugh and continued, 'Swanington must be prepared for some damage, even some thieving.'

Jemima could not deny the risk he had to take.

He seemed to be thinking out loud when he said, 'We can accommodate the Londoners in tents in the large paddock away from the house. My men and I will keep an eye on them. As they are doing a job for me, I shall do my best to make their stay here comfortable — but not so comfortable that they will overstay their welcome.'

'Bravo!' said the countess. 'I was hoping you would conclude thus.'

William smiled at his grandmother and said, 'I am comforted to know you agree with my decision, Grandmama.' He then turned to Jemima. 'I will ask you to take great care to protect yourself and my grandmother during this coming storm.'

'Of course I will!' retorted Jemima, but remembering she still had to talk to him about her independence, she added, 'However, I cannot be shut up here like a prisoner! I am too confined. I need to be free to come and go — '

'You need to be safe!' William raised his voice and his steely eyes bore into hers. 'You will do as I say. I cannot prevent my relatives from insulting you, but I intend to protect you as best I can. As for your London visitors, you will know best how to deal with them and I shall overlook their behaviour with the help of my staff. But Dykes — ah! He is a different matter! As my bride-to-be you will be danger until he is captured.'

Jemima bristled and she refused to

blink as she gave him a response to his dictate. Lifting her chin, she retorted, 'We are not married yet, William. I will do as I think best. When my visitors come from London I shall want to mingle among them. I do not intend to shut myself up in my room just in case Dykes takes a pot-shot at me!'

William was breathing heavily, his hands clenched and unclenched as he strove to control his anger. 'I will see that you do as I say!'

At this point in the confrontation the countess rose sharply, saying, 'I will retire now and leave you two to sort out your differences. If you desire my opinion I would say you are both right and you cannot prevent what will be — only take precautions, as I am sure you both will.'

Jemima and William rose to their feet and bowed to the older lady as she swept out of the room with a slight nod and smile for each of them.

Jemima immediately felt uncomfortable that she had not kissed the countess goodnight, but she understood why she and William had been left alone so promptly, without even calling for her maid to see her upstairs to bed. It was their very relationship they were deciding — their future.

Left alone, like two stags with their antlers down ready to butt each other, Jemima recognised an impasse between them. She was prepared to marry him and accept being his wife, but because of her independent background, she would not — could not — become an obedient wife in *all* things.

She could not accept a life of docility, doing as she was told. She had been independent in London — which held far more dangers than here in the west country. Of course, Dykes was still a threat to both of them, but she was dealing with the matter, was she not?

Left standing when the dowager had left the room, Jemima was able to review her assessment of her intended. Taller than her, she had to look up at him, and admire his physical appearance. She knew what he looked like unclothed, and his figure was as perfect as a Greek statue. His tailor, and new valet, had dressed him so that he looked the epitome of an English gentleman attired in his evening clothes. His cravat was not showy but correct in every detail. His evening shoes had silver buckles that gleamed — like his fierce expression in the candlelight.

His countenance was, at present, harsh. He had matured to become a man of mental and physical strength.

But Jemima was armed with knowledge about his vulnerability. His sense of responsibility for his inheritance and his care for those under him he took seriously. He shared their joys and their sorrows. That was why he was upset this evening, knowing some of his families were grieving because their men folk were paying the price of smuggling with his rotten valet who had led them astray when he as earl should have been more vigilant. He should have spotted Dykes was up to no good long before he did, and so possibly saved the life of his maid.

Oh yes, he had broad enough shoulders to take all he had to bear, but he needed support. His grandmother, his friends, and his loyal servants gave him that. But Jemima, looking at him, knew her presence was of importance to him — as indeed he was to her.

Coming closer to him as if drawn like a moth to a flame, she held out her hands, saying, 'Come, William, let us not quarrel. Our aims are exactly the same — to catch Dykes before he does any more harm, and to run your estate for the benefit of all. I have an unruly crowd coming to destroy the peace for a while but I shall endeavour to control them — if you will allow me to do so and not lock me up!'

His face relaxed into a smile as his large hands took hers. He raised her fingers to his lips. Then his eyes looked up from his bow and she saw something in them she had never seen before — an intense look, a raw desire for her.

Never having experienced the urge

for a man to kiss her so strongly, to want him to crush her to his body, Jemima almost panted with desire as he scattered little kisses all over her face, neck and bosom. The colour in her cheeks reddened.

His voice croaked a little before he stopped kissing her suddenly, stepped away from her and cleared this throat.

'Jemima, I do not wish to curtail your freedom — heaven forbid! I know you too well to know that would be impossible!'

She smiled, loving the way he held her hands and gave her fingers a squeeze. He bent to kiss her again lightly and whisper in her ear.

'You must understand, it is because I love you that I could not bear for any harm to come to you. I want you to be protected until Dykes is captured. That is why I am so intent to make sure you are not an easy target for him by wandering around with no protection. You must stay safe for me.'

Was he feeling the same urge to clasp

her tight again as she was feeling? Did his body tingle with desire for her? Yes, she felt sure they both needed to make love now. But she knew they must not.

They were in his grandmother's house, servants were around — and they were not yet married.

Jemima understood a man's need was great when aroused, so in fairness to him, she had to break away, swiftly turning from him and releasing her hands from his grasp.

'It is late. You have had an awful day and we are expecting visitors of sorts, William. We will both need our rest to cope with them.'

She did not watch his expression, just felt the tug on her fingers as he tried to hold onto her hand, but he was a noble man and let her go.

Before leaving the room he bowed to her.

'Forgive my attempts to ensure you are kept safe, Jemima. I know you are a sensible young lady and I should leave it to your judgment to protect yourself in the coming weeks — however long it takes to get Dykes.'

As he shut the door after him, she felt the horror of him being injured again — killed, even — and called after him, 'Look after yourself, William.'

He had gone before she could add, *I love you*.

Now she had her wish to be free from so many constraints, Jemima suddenly felt vulnerable. Dykes may be hiding anywhere in or around Swanington. She had not really thought of it before — and should have — but had her wish to do as she pleased added to William's burden?

# 16

Despite the quiet, orderly life at Swanington Dower House, Jemima was getting used to busily preparing for her wedding and planning to move into the palatial Swanington Hall. She foresaw pandemonium immediately ahead.

Having the burden of knowing it was her suggestion that an unruly mob should come to Swanington to search for Dykes, when she heard from her brother Charles, and definitely knew they were coming, she sent a message up to the Hall asking William to call at the Dower House.

Seeing him dismount from his thoroughbred, her heart lurched. How magnificent he looked in his well-tailored country clothes. From his hat, worn at a slightly rakish angle, down to his highly polished Hessians, he looked unmistakably the impressive Earl of Swanington.

With a purposeful walk he crunched

over the gravelled drive towards the front door of the Dower House where Jemima rushed to greet him.

Regardless of servants who might be watching, William's eyes sought hers as his tall form came close to her. Removing his hat and riding crop, he passed them to the ever-attentive butler, Sprott.

Sprott bowed saying. 'Good day, your lordship.'

'Good morning, Sprott. Is my grand-mother well?' William asked.

'Yes, sir. Taking life a little easier these days.'

'Good. Perhaps you will tell her that as I am here I would like to pay my respects.'

'Most certainly, sir,' replied Sprott, bowing before disappearing into the house with the earl's belongings to leave Jemima outside with him.

The pair were left alone outside the house. Jemima felt a little overawed at William's show of powerful manhood at its peak of perfection. She felt herself surprisingly shy.

He looked at her appreciatively. 'You look delicious — I could eat you!'

She was pleased to know her choice of gown was successful — heaven knows she had spent enough time trying to decide what to wear that morning, and her new sprigged cotton was chosen with care. Peggy was learning her trade from the other ladies' maids and could dress her hair prettily. Even her shoes with their low heels clicked femininely as she walked to him.

'William,' she whispered, 'I am sorry to have called for you when I know you must be very busy.'

'I am glad you did, Jemima. I am engrossed in my duties, it is true, but my heart is always with you. I long for your kisses — so give me one now!'

It was outrageous for him to ask her to come into his arms in front of the house with servants able to see them embrace. But Jemima was not embarrassed, for her only thoughts were of delight to be the woman he had chosen and wanted.

His almost savage grasping of her body and his hungry kiss took her breath away. But she melted, the scent of his skin and sandalwood soap, and the freshness of his linen. The exquisite touch of his lips on hers, his hands stroking her body . . .

Pulling away, she gasped, 'Come into the house, William. You are ruining my reputation!'

The Earl chuckled as he released her.

With his arm around her slender form, they entered the house, stepping into the hall where two giggling maids curtsied to them as they passed into the drawing room.

'I would dearly love to spend the morning with you,' he said releasing her with a rueful smile. 'But I must make other calls today.'

Knowing the vast area of his estates and the pressures on him she smiled up at him, although her lips quivered. She did not want him to leave, especially as he might be walking into danger. He was like a soldier going into battle with a sniper waiting to kill him! But like a soldier's sweetheart she had to part with him and be brave about it.

She said, 'I know you have much to do, but I asked you to come as I would like you to read this letter from my brother, Charles.' Picking up the reticule hanging from her waist on a chain, she removed the letter and gave it to him.

Giving the missive all his attention, William read it. Then he laughed.

'Hey ho! We are in for a storm! Charles is certainly warning us about what is to come — and it certainly frightens me — and let us hope it frightens Dykes, too, if he is still in the neighbourhood.'

'Who will organise the search?'

'I will. I know every nook and cranny of Swanington — but unfortunately, so does Dykes.'

Jemima nodded but said, 'The London people coming are like bloodhounds. I am certain they will find him — if indeed he is still around here.'

They looked at each other with a

deep understanding of the grave situation.

When she tried to describe to him who to expect to arrive from London, he listened patiently.

'I fear they will be a motley crew. Some of them may have been the thieves who robbed you that night you fell off the coach,' she warned, and then added in a nervous, hushed voice as she thought of it, 'And how do we know they may not help themselves to the Hall's gold and silver?'

'I shall get the servants to lock away the most precious Swanington treasures.'

Another concern struck her. 'They are due the day after tomorrow. Where are you going to house them all?'

William squared his shoulders. 'I have consulted my estate manager and we have discussed the problem. My men, and the Hall servants are aware of the invasion. And let us not forget my relatives, who are sure to be a right royal pain in the neck!' He grimaced.

'My aunt and uncle will be housed in the west wing, well away from the London crowd.'

His ability to govern his estate, to deal with the problem confronting him was becoming evident.

'There are some barns on the estate that have been cleaned for them to holiday in. Or some may set up tents I have borrowed from the army in the large meadow.'

Jemima smiled, and then frowned. 'What about feeding them all?'

'My estate manager and housekeeper have arranged for a camp kitchen to be set up.'

Jemima sighed with relief. The problem of accommodation had been solved, and William seemed quite reconciled to the prospect of his estate being invaded.

'Thank you, William,' she said giving him a kiss. 'I just hope they will behave.'

'I just hope they capture Dykes!' he replied.

They looked at each other with a solemn expression, for the thought of being stalked and attacked by Dykes was never far from his — or her — mind.

'Before I go,' he said, 'I must go up and see my beloved grandmama — and kiss you again.' He swept Jemima into an embrace. With his strong hands firmly placed at the top of her arms, he looked down into her eyes, saying hoarsely, 'You will look after her, won't you, Jemima?'

'Of course, I will. I love her as you do, William.'

What should have been a quick kiss goodbye turned into a lingering moment of passion.

Jemima no longer hid her desire for him. Her fingers went around the back of his neck to press herself close to him. His lips caught hers with a hungry need.

'William,' she murmured, 'I love you. Take care of yourself. Do not try to be a hero — you shall have many people helping you to bring Dykes to justice.'

'And you too, Jemima, must take the greatest care because Dykes is impatient to nail us both.'

They hugged for some time. Parting was hard to do, but necessary. Jemima knew she must let him go to work — she had kept him too long.

Their enemy was only one man, but a sniper could be deadly — and Dykes had several advantages. He knew Swanington and he was a skilled impersonator.

* * *

Vengeance kept Dykes in the neighbourhood.

He could have left the district weeks ago if he had not been greedy and wanted to stay for the last haul. Now it was too late. He was riddled with fury that his lucrative smuggling business was at an end. The youthful Earl of Swanington, whom he had dressed for years, had ceased to be a fluffy cygnet and become a fully grown swan capable of attacking him.

When he had to kill that interfering maid, Dykes had thought it easy to put the blame for the murder on the young earl.

That was his first mistake.

William, Earl of Swanington, had a grandmother who had protected him from the law when he had been accused. Then, the earl's friends had proved that his lordship was miles away when the murder was committed — therefore, the Earl of Swanington was no longer sought by the law for murder.

It was a pity they had not found and hanged his lordship quickly.

So now the hunt for the killer was ongoing. But worse than that, the earl had taken up the challenge to find the killer himself.

The second mistake Dykes made was to have set up the capture of the earl and then not kill him after he had caught him.

The other smugglers had refused to

finish him off, and he had been left tied up with that young woman of his — who he had been hoodwinked into thinking was another maid.

That was his third mistake, for they had wriggled themselves free and now were after him.

The lawmen had found and taken his hoard of smuggled goods and had captured his men, who were now languishing in jail. Only he had been clever enough to give the constables the slip.

But because he had boasted he had killed the maid, he was wanted for murder as well as smuggling. Dykes now had practically nothing left to show now for his years of expert smuggling business — except that he wanted to do something violent or harmful to the Earl of Swanington and his bride-to-be.

He knew he would have to remove himself from the district and start his illegal trade somewhere else, but he would have the satisfaction of knowing he had got his own back of the Earl of

Swanington and that woman of his, who he heard had hired some London coves to find him.

He had to keep hidden from the Hall's staff and estate workers who knew him — but he could dress up and act as if he were an old, bearded man to beg for food, find a corner in a hay barn to sleep, strike when it suited him — then run off where no one could find him.

Vindictive and cruel under his polished valet's manner, Uriah Dykes was the slipperiest of enemies.

He had heard some servants talk of a manhunt for him — they were going to ship in men from London to assist the local constables. What a laugh that would be! Watching them because he had been disguised, able to observe their vain attempt to track him down, until they gave up, thinking he had left the area, and then they would return to London. He would get the better of them all — he would not have to persuade his men to kill William this time — he would do it himself.

It did not occur to him that he had made mistakes in the past and was likely to make more.

# 17

The sun shone brightly from early morning — a perfect haymaking day. As the shire horses were harnessed and the men and women haymakers assembled to gather their pitch forks and walk in procession to the long grass fields, ready to be mowed, and the grass collected to provide feed for the animals in wintertime, Jemima rose to prepare herself for a busy day.

While the blackbirds trilled their sweet tunes outside, Peggy informed her that her new day gown was ready to wear and insisted she put on the pretty sprigged cotton.

'There, Miss, it fits you just right,' she said admiringly, when the highwaisted light cotton gown was laced down Jemima's back, showing her slender female form to perfection. The freshness of the garment and the manner in which Peggy dressed her hair was pleasing.

The first visitors to arrive at Swanington were cartloads of noisy Londoners, accompanied by Jemima's brother, Charles, who explained he had decided to take a holiday and had accompanied them to Devon. The well-travelled Mr Charles Perrot had hired a private chaise and driver to take him in comfort to Swanington. However, he was not too lofty to avoid travelling with the Londoners, and made sure none of them got lost among the narrow winding country lanes.

Kissing his sister, who had come to the Hall to greet him, Charles explained, 'A jaunt like this is a break from my town shop. I miss journeying abroad and around China — and I wanted to congratulate you on your engagement, Jemima. Society is abuzz with the news that the Earl of Swanington has chosen a bride. Although I do not have much to tell them about it, other than she is my sister. So I thought to pay a visit. I hope his lordship does not mind me inviting myself?'

William was pleased to see him, and shook his hand warmly. 'You are welcome, brother Charles. I could do with a good-natured fellow like yourself at the Hall to help cope with my relatives who are due to arrive soon. And you are a master at dealing with disgruntled customers — as Jemima and I fear they will be.'

'I shall do my best, your lordship. I would rather deal with your relatives than that lot.'

He pointed to the motley crowd of Londoners, who looked overawed at the size of the Hall and the curious servants who had come outside to gape at the unusual crowd of visitors.

The Londoners were not at a loss for long — the children from the City were the first to make themselves at home, jumping off the carts and running about in delight, screeching, until their elders began to collar them when they had also climbed down from their carts.

'Show them to their camp site and give them some refreshment,' boomed the Earl to his servants, seeming to accept them all by striding over and shaking hands with his assorted guests.

A little dog was soon dancing around his feet barking joyfully.

'M'Harty, my friend!' exclaimed William bending down to stroke him.

Sure enough, there was Blind Joe holding onto his wife's arm.

Jemima ran to hug them. Overwhelmed to be reunited with the people she knew, tears formed in her eyes. She and William needed help, and so many had come after her call for assistance. One or two of the more obvious bruisers she felt less pleased to see, but she thought Dykes would not be pleased to see them either.

Peggy was there among them, squawking happily to the people from the streets she knew. 'Her folk', she called them, as she welcomed them and helped to serve refreshments.

So while Mr Charles Perrot and his luggage were taken into the Hall and he was shown his rooms by a footman, Jemima assured him she had to see the

Londoners settle into their quarters and would see him later.

Much to Jemima's relief, the Londoners seemed delighted with the camping ground allocated to them.

'It's loverly!' many of the women declared.

After living their lives in the grimy streets of London, it was not surprising the countryside appeared heavenly — and for many it was the first time they had seen lush green pasture and trees.

A little later, William, Earl of Swanington, having helped his guests settle into their tents, stood up on a fallen log in the camp site to address the Londoners.

'I would like the men to meet me on the terrace at six o'clock, after you have settled in,' he ordered, clearly taking command and wanting to get on with the purpose for their coming.

Having settled the travellers into their outdoor accommodation, and seeing them contented, as well as the cart horses being fed and watered, Jemima began to walk back towards the Hall, anxious to see her brother.

She had not gone far when she heard William calling after her.

'Wait!'

Jemima turned to see him running after her and when he came nearer she could see he seemed displeased.

Panting, he boomed at her, 'Where the hell do you think you are going?'

His rudeness made Jemima's heart thump and she stood wondering what had upset him.

There was something almost frightening about the size and strength of him that made Jemima gasp. A male power that attracted her and mesmerised her to stand still and allow him to approach her, dominate her.

'I am going to see my brother, Charles,' she replied with a frown.

He was now gripping her shoulders, 'You cannot go by yourself!'

She bristled and her eyes flashed at him.

'Do I have to ask your permission to go to your house? Or do you think that because I am engaged to you that I am your property now, for you to say what I should and should not do?'

It was not the most tactful thing to have said. Seeing the anger increase on his face, she immediately regretted saying it.

He had put himself out to be congenial to her London visitors, many of whom he would, under normal circumstances, do his best to avoid. And she was being petty, too quick to find fault with him, when in fact she was at fault.

It took her a few moments to realise he was angry because he was afraid for her safety. So afraid, indeed, that he lost his temper. All those people had just arrived from London to seek the murderer who had almost killed them both, and here she was striding off towards the Hall when the evil valet could nab her at any moment, perhaps use her as a hostage! Of course he thought she should have servants to escort her.

William said firmly, 'You promised me you would be careful where you went and what you did. And look at you — out in the open, a perfect target for Dykes!'

Tears formed in her eyes, as she blinked rapidly. 'I did not think-'

'You must think!'

She was temporarily unable to respond and she turned her face away from him. Did he really think she was lacking in common sense? Pressing her lips together hard she ought to admit she was in the wrong, but hearing him ranting did not help.

'I have enough to do organising the hunt for Dykes. Where is your maid, Peggy?'

Her voice went quiet. 'You know Peggy is with her friends at the camp. She is so delighted to see them, I can hardly ask her to abandon them. After they have come all this way and she is enjoying seeing them again.'

'You could have asked another servant to escort you.'

'There were none about, and I truly did not give it a thought!'

They stood and glared at each other.

William shook his head running his fingers through his hair as if he was deeply stressed.

'Good God, woman! Do you want to get us both killed?' He made an exasperated sigh. 'The least you can do to help me is to do what you can to protect yourself by having people around when you go abroad. Is that too much to ask?'

Struck by the horrid thought that she had put not only herself at risk, but him too, Jemima said, 'I am sorry, William. You must understand that I am so used to being able go where I please, when I please. Having to consider any danger around at every minute is not constantly on my mind.'

He shook his head. 'It is surely not much to ask you to keep some servants near you.'

'I suppose it is not.'

Jemima was cross with herself now. She was not helping William at all when she should be. She was flattered that he thought so much of her that he seemed worried sick about her safety, but she did not like him losing his temper with her.

'William,' she said, 'I have said I am sorry. I made a mistake and — '

'Well, in case you make another, I shall assign bodyguards to be around you at all times.'

How awful to be spied on constantly — and by men! Jemima's rebellious spirit made her protest.

'No! I shall not be watched night and day!'

'Oh, yes, you shall!'

She snapped back, 'You are just as vulnerable to attack as I — so where are *your* bodyguards?'

'Look over by the trees.'

Sure enough, when she turned around Jemima saw the shapes of men half hidden but able to watch. She swallowed hard, conscious of her error, and said, 'I am truly sorry, William.'

She brushed the tears from her eyes with her fingers and sniffed, trying to control her tears.

He kicked the toe of his polished boot into the grass saying, 'Believe me, Jemima, I understand how irritating it must be for you to be constantly watched, but it *is* necessary. Dykes is no ordinary criminal, he has the ability to disguise himself as you know, and he can choose his time and place to attack. We are at his mercy until he is caught.'

She gave a shudder, suddenly feeling afraid. 'I know ... I know that, William.'

'Then please take more care. I am sorry to have frightened you. I only want to impress upon you the danger you are in — that we are both in.'

William calmed a little as they walked towards the imposing front of Swanington Hall, and he explained quickly what Jemima was to expect from his relatives.

'Cousin Clarence is my heir, and my father's nephew. Being much older than me, even though we were at Eton together, we never had the desire to be friends.' He took a breath, hissing between his teeth, 'To be honest, he is not my sort.'

Jemima looked up at his set expression and wondered what kind of man Clarence could be as William's expression appeared worried.

He continued, 'His mother, my Aunt Josephina, is a formidable woman.'

'Oh dear!' exclaimed Jemima before she could check her feelings of trepidation.

'Even her husband, Uncle Augustus, has little to recommend him in my eyes.'

'I hope you have accommodated them well away from our London guests.'

'The housekeeper has given them the North Wing — so their suite of rooms are not anywhere near the others.'

He squared his shoulders and Jemima thought he looked like a soldier prepared for battle. He was now far from being the scared boy at the mercy of his unkind relatives — as they would soon find out.

'I hate to have to remind you, Jemima, that Dykes will be like a hunted animal and all the more dangerous for that. Please do not go into the woods or down to the beach until he is caught. I would ask you to stay indoors.'

'I will,' she said, and meaning it. She stretched up to give his check a light kiss, before giving him a smile and dutiful curtsey.

# 18

Dinner at Swanington Hall when entertaining visitors was a grand affair. The servants had spent considerable time bringing out the best china, polishing the silver, and arranging the flowers and napkins. The cooks in the steamy kitchens were preparing a fine meal, the footmen put on their best liveries, and the maids changed into clean pinafores ready to serve the food. They were happy to be able to make the Hall shine as it did when William's parents were alive.

The Dowager Lady Swanington had kindly agreed to act as the gracious hostess as she had been for many years when the hall was her home. Her knowledge of protocol for these occasions was invaluable for making the occasion run smoothly, and it enabled Jemima to learn the role she would be taking in future as the countess. Not that Jemima or William would keep to the old style of lavish entertaining, which was far too extravagant and formal for them. But on this occasion they were as excited as their staff to play their part in the formal dinner for their guests.

Attired in a beautiful silk gown and holding the fan Jemima had given her, the countess played the role of hostess graciously. She had played it hundreds of times when she was younger and her husband, the late Earl was alive. Her old eyes sparkled like her tiara, set in her snow-white hair, as she quietly set an example for Jemima of the art of being a charming hostess.

After the two ladies arrived at the Hall and were kissed by William, they sat waiting for their guests to appear downstairs.

Jemima said to Lady Swanington behind her fan. 'Having you here, ma'am, gives me courage.'

'My dear Jemima, you have plenty of that. You have nothing to fear from

William's relatives. Just be yourself. However badly they behave, they have no right to be here. You are now family as much as they are.'

Jemima was content that she looked the part of the future countess. Peggy had dressed her with the utmost care in her white silk evening dress — a beautiful example of dressmaking by one of the top London mantua makers — and even William's aunt would be forced to admire it. Her youthful neckline, with her hair combed up to reveal its slenderness, was enhanced by the necklace William had given her. And her exquisite engagement ring would shine in the candlelight so that none could deny she was the Earl's bride.

★   ★   ★

The portly figure of Uncle Augustus and his wife, the birdlike Aunt Josephina, approached her with critical expressions on their faces. Clearly they thought themselves to be full of importance, and were

293

aiming to make it clear to Jemima that they did not approve of her.

Their son was no better. Cousin Clarence was a weedy young man with no conversation or congratulations for Jemima. She was thankful Tom Corbishire and her brother Charles were there as their social manners kept him entertained — and well away from her.

It was after dinner when they were having coffee in the saloon that Aunt Josephina, who had ignored Jemima for most of the evening, sidled up to her and sat on a chair in front of her.

She announced spitefully, 'I expect you are aware, Miss Perrot, that my nephew is accused of murder! And indeed if you look at him, it is clear he has been in some kind of drunken brawl.'

Jemima hid a gasp. Then she caught sight of the Dowager Duchess fanning herself rapidly. Glancing over at the grand lady, Jemima saw the lady wink at her. Immediately Jemima realised she must rise to the challenge of being bullied.

Smiling at Aunt Josephina, she replied quite cheerfully, 'Yes, indeed. William has been caught up in trouble recently. As I was just a year ago.'

Aunt Josphina's sharp eyes seemed like pins pricking her, and she was more than a little put out in realising that Jemima was not the kind of young lady she could easily frighten.

Jemima added, 'William has a temper, I grant you, but he has a heart of gold.'

Clearly unsure what Jemima meant by that remark, Aunt Josephina continued, 'William's maid was slaughtered and we know not if William was the killer. It is only fair to tell you that Augustus and I have always thought him a pampered youth capable of anything. Not like our Clarence, who would make a fine Earl.'

This statement was outside of propriety, but Jemima took it in her stride. Daintily she drank the last of her coffee and leisurely put her cup down on a nearby table.

'Oh, you have not heard then,

ma'am? The murderer is known. It was William's valet. Indeed, he is being hunted at this very moment, and there are men all over the estate searching for him. So you must not be surprised if you meet some unsavoury characters in the gardens, or if you hear or come across their urchins playing about the grounds.'

That information seemed to take Aunt Josephina by horror as well as surprise. She looked around uneasily. 'Who are these rough men?'

'My friends, from where I used to live in the London Docklands. William hired them to find his evil valet.'

Jemima was aware that she was telling her secret about living in a poor area of London to a lady who would be sure to repeat it — but she no longer cared. She felt sure the women in the Docklands were as good as Aunt Josephina — indeed, most were far better.

Once more Lady Swanington's fan was fluttering rapidly and Jemima's attention was caught by it. This time the dowager was giving her a warning, not to say more about her background. The lady's finger was placed on her lips behind her fan.

Jemima was amused and almost laughed, but she accepted she must be careful what she said to Aunt Josephina — and certainly must not allow herself to be carried away and become careless in her chatter. She had shown she was capable of rising above the aunt's taunts. It would not be wise to go so far as to make an enemy of William's relatives.

However, she was saved from doing that as Mary Corbishire glided up and, putting her arm around Jemima, kissed her check saying, 'Your brother, Charles, has gifted me this beautiful fan. He said you asked him to bring me one from his shop. I must thank you.'

Mary spread out the fan before the ladies to show the exquisite Chinese workmanship.

Admiring it, Jemima was able to

assure Aunt Josephina that her brother could obtain one for her too, which seemed to please her, because evening fans were very popular and Charles's new shop was renowned for stocking the very best fans in London.

★ ★ ★

William kept Jemima at the Hall for a few minutes after his guests retired, before returning her and his grandmother to the Dower House. Escorting her into the library on the pretext that he wanted to find a book of poetry for her, he closed the door behind him with his evening-slippered foot, and took her into his arms to kiss her goodnight.

'You look truly beautiful this evening, my darling Jemima. You made my heart glow with pride looking at you.'

'And you, my lord, in your evening dress — it made me love you more than I do already.'

Indeed, his formal blue dress coat with black velvet collar, cream waistcoat and knee breeches, were most becoming on the young man.

'I noticed you are wearing the necklace I gave you,' he murmured, kissing her ear and neck.

Jemima kissed his scarred cheek. 'It happens to be the only one I have — but even if I possessed many necklaces I would always like it best. As indeed I love the engagement ring you gave me.'

They kissed again until Jemima whispered, 'I must go and not keep your grandmother waiting.'

★ ★ ★

Back in the Dower House undressing in her room later that evening, Jemima felt a sense of achievement on realising that, like William, she had changed, grown in confidence. She had developed more skill in dealing not only with the rough and tumble Londoners, but also those in a high position in Society — which would be useful in her

future role as the Countess of Swanington.

About to climb into bed, she paused
on hearing loud, continuous rapping on
her chamber door.

'Who's there?' she called apprehen-
sively.

Peggy immediately burst into the
room.

It seemed like a repeat performance
to be called in the late hours of the evening
by her maid, and remembering what
had happened the last time when she
had ventured out to Swanington Mill,
Jemima felt she was not keen to leave
her bedroom to go on an rescue errand
if she was asked to this time.

'Peggy,' she said. 'Please calm yourself.'

The candle Peggy carried illuminated
her agitated expression as she blurted
out, 'I was told to tell you that
Dykes . . . ' She faltered and gave a
visible shudder.

'Put that candle down, Peggy, or you
may drop it and set the house on fire.'

'Yes, miss.'

Peggy had yet to learn to call her mistress ma'am, not miss, but this was not the time to correct the maid as she was obviously upset. Dykes had harmed her, and she was afraid.

Trying to remain unruffled herself, Jemima asked, 'What about Dykes?'

'I've been told to tell you, 'e's been spotted, on the estate.'

Jemima felt her heart thump uncomfortably.

'Who told you to tell me that?'

'His lordship. 'e said I was to go to you and stay with you. And some of the 'all servants are 'ere downstairs to make sure her ladyship and you are all right.'

Jemima breathed more easily to learn that Peggy had brought some men to guard them, but she was still anxious to know more of what was going on. She asked, 'What exactly do you mean, that Dykes has been spotted?'

Peggy, who had put the candlestick down on the dressing table, sat down heavily on a bedroom chair without being told she could. Jemima over-looked the lack of manners in her servant as it was clear that Peggy was as worried as she had also become.

Peggy explained, 'I mean that cruel man was seen by some boys from the camp this evening. Down on the beach, they said they saw him, in some caves they was playing in.'

Jemima realised that Dykes could well have a den hidden in the caves, and the boys could have discovered it. But then she thought out loud. 'So has he been captured?'

Jemima's heart sank when Peggy shook her head. 'No, 'e'd gone by the time the boys 'ad raced back and told the men.'

Learning Dykes was still on the loose and in the neighbourhood was a blow to her. Then she thought of poor William learning the news and being as distraught as she felt — as well as having the responsibility of trying to protect a houseful of guests and servants, his mother and betrothed from the dangerous criminal.

The Hall and the estate and nearby villages covered a vast area. And for a man who knew it as well as Dykes did, finding a new hiding place would not be difficult. Although an army of people were searching for him, it was night time now and like a wily, hunted animal, Dykes would not be easily found.

Jemima's mouth felt dry. She asked Peggy if she would light her candle for her, then go downstairs and get her a drink. 'A dish of tea, if you please, Peggy.'

Peggy seemed pleased to have something to do, but when she had gone, Jemima wished she had not. In the dark room the candle spluttered in the draughts, making the room seem full of dancing shadows. Being alone she felt vulnerable, afraid to think of a killer prowling about.

No wonder William had sent her maid to be with her! *It was silly of me to send Peggy down to the kitchen for some tea, but she will be back soon*, she told herself firmly.

To take her mind off the uneasy feeling she had, Jemima went to her closet and took out a robe. Covering her nightgown, she sat at her dressing table and began to tidy some of her toilet things.

A bang behind her made her start. The bedroom door was flung open.

'Peggy, please!' she cried in annoyance, 'If the household is not awake already you will rouse them all by making a noise like that.'

However, when she turned she saw it was not Peggy at the door, but William standing in the darkness of the corridor. He was still attired in his formal evening wear, looking very commanding.

'Oh William, I am so pleased to see you, even though you gave me a nasty shock!' she said, rising and walking towards the door to greet him.

A sudden shout from the window made her eyes swivel round to see another man, dressed exactly the same, opening her bedroom window — he looked like William, too!

Her mind felt all in a jumble and her mouth fell open in shock. Which one was William?

'Jemima! Over here,' said the man at the door.

'Stay there!' ordered the man at the window.

Confused, she realised that one of the men was William, her beloved — and the other was Dykes, the man who could kill her!

Jemima froze.

How could she decide who was the real earl in the light of just one candle? Painful seconds of uncertainty went by as she looked from one figure to the next. Surely the Earl of Swanington would come though the door, not come clambering through the window like a burglar?

Oh, which one was Dykes? She knew he had been the earl's valet and he had access to his clothes and had worn them before to trick her and capture her.

Struck by the dreadful situation that she might make a mistake and walk to the man who would harm her, she clasped her hands tightly together drawing them up to her lips to prevent herself from screaming. Dykes could capture her, hold her and hurt her, blackmail William. Her mind whirled with the harm that man had inflicted on others and could still do it.

Trembling, Jemima fought her scrambled senses to think how could she discover which of those two men was Dykes. Suddenly something came into her mind . . . a little yappy dog . . . and only one of the men would know its name.

Breathing with difficulty she looked at the well-dressed gentleman in the door frame, and asked him, 'Tell me the name of Blind Joe's dog.'

She received no answer.

The man at the window climbed in. Holding a pistol in his hand and pointing it directly at the figure at the door, he said, 'Joe's dog is M'harty.'

Now she knew!

The presence of William behind her was comforting, especially now that men could be heard shouting as they pounded up the stairs.

Dykes made a dive forward.

William immediately stood in front of Jemima to protect her, dropping his pistol as he did so. The duelling pistol skidded across the wooden floor and Jemima screamed — Dykes could easily pick it up and shoot William! Her horror at knowing William would be his target made Jemima feel faint as she watched the snarling Dykes.

As the men behind him had reached the landing and were running to capture him, Dykes leapt forward with a piercing yell.

Jemima closed her eyes, expecting them to be attacked, but he rushed by them and raced to the open window and threw himself out of it!

Men crowded into her bedchamber, some followed Dykes out through the window, shouting, 'After him!'

A few minutes later all the men were

gone, chasing after Dykes.

Sobbing with fright, Jemima allowed William to comfort her as he said softly, 'Do not concern yourself any longer, my darling Jemima. There is a pack of hunters after Dykes now and he will not get away this time.'

Held tightly in his arms as William kissed her, her anguish melted away.

* * *

In the morning, the countess did not remark about her grandson having breakfast at her house instead of at the Hall. Indeed, she did not appear to know anything about what had gone on in her home overnight — or she was tactful enough not to mention anything about it.

Jemima was grateful. She had already learned many useful lessons from the countess, and being silent about what she knew was sometimes, she realised, for the best.

'What are you planning to do today?'

Jemima asked William, putting down her cup of coffee and taking another warm muffin onto her plate to butter. She felt tired and hungry after the horrendous events of the previous evening.

William had eaten a hearty breakfast too, and now sat back on his chair looking a picture of contentment. He replied, 'I must now persuade all our guests to leave,' he added with a chuckle.

'Which party?' asked his grand-mother.

'All of 'em!' William laughed. 'I must also tell you that Dykes has left us for good.'

Jemima shivered at the mention of the name. With wide eyes she asked, 'How do you know?'

'My new valet came over to the Dower House early this morning with my shaving things and some clean clothes for me. He told me the news.'

Jemima and the countess looked at him expectantly, so he continued,

'Apparently Dykes raced down to the beach with a pack of hunters behind him. He tried to reach his hideaway, but was cut off by the tide . . . '

He need say no more. Drowning seemed an appropriate end to a cruel man who had caused so much grief.

★   ★   ★

It was a day later that the grand exit from Swanington took place.

Aunt Josephina and Uncle Augustus went off in an elegant coach with Cousin Clarence riding beside it, looking less belligerent than when they had arrived.

William had done his best to soften them up without losing his temper with his relatives.

The Londoners left earlier as they had a long, slow journey by horse and cart ahead of them. They appeared to have more baggage with them than they arrived with, but it was not mentioned.

Jemima kissed Blind Joe and his wife, and his little dog, M'harty, received a stroke from her and from William too.

Seeing the heavily laden carts swaying as they disappeared into the distance, the Earl of Swanington put his arm around Jemima and said cheerfully, 'That scurvy lot have robbed me of half my fortune!'

Jemima, who stood beside him, smiled.

The valuable purse those Londoner thieves had stolen from him when he had fallen from the coach, together with what they had purloined recently during their stay at Swanington, as well as the recompense he had paid to those on his estate who claimed they had possessions taken, broken or missing, must have cost him a small fortune.

She looked up at him, knowing he had suffered a great deal in one way or another since she had first seen him. However, he was undoubtedly as happy as she felt.

His eyes looked at her lovingly as he said, 'Yet for all I have suffered and lost,

I have gained a priceless treasure — you, Jemima.'

The Dowager Countess, who had come to see the visitors depart, smiled indulgently and walked away tactfully when her grandson took his betrothed into his arms and kissed her passionately.

We do hope that you have enjoyed reading this large print book.

Did you know that all of our titles are available for purchase?

We publish a wide range of high quality large print books including:
**Romances, Mysteries, Classics**
**General Fiction**
**Non Fiction and Westerns**

Special interest titles available in large print are:
**The Little Oxford Dictionary**
**Music Book, Song Book**
**Hymn Book, Service Book**

Also available from us courtesy of Oxford University Press:
**Young Readers' Dictionary**
**(large print edition)**
**Young Readers' Thesaurus**
**(large print edition)**

For further information or a free brochure, please contact us at:
**Ulverscroft Large Print Books Ltd.,**
**The Green, Bradgate Road, Anstey,**
**Leicester, LE7 7FU, England.**
**Tel:** (00 44) **0116 236 4325**
**Fax:** (00 44) **0116 234 0205**